Canvas
Of a Mind

PURBA CHAKRABORTY

First published in 2017 by

Becomeshakespeare.com
Wordit Content Design & Editing Services Pvt Ltd
Unit - 26, Building A-1, Nr Wadala RTO, Wadala (East),
Mumbai 400037, India
T:+91 8080226699

©
ISBN: 978-93-86487-22-3

DEDICATION

To Disha, my beloved cousin. I love you, precious. You will always stay in my heart.
(Disha Ganguly—20 June 1992 to 9 April 2015)

ACKNOWLEDGEMENTS

Without some wonderful people, this book wouldn't have been possible. I would like to take this opportunity to thank those people who have been with me during the making of this book.

First of all, I would like to thank my Dad and Grandmother for their support. Whenever my chips were down, my Dad's motivating words helped me get back on my feet with renewed enthusiasm.

I also owe this book to our family trip to Kalimpong in 2015 which formed the backdrop of the novel. I have met some interesting people while traveling who inspired some of the characters of the book.

I would like to thank my soul sister, Priyam for being the first reader of my books. I shared the idea of this book first with her and how I loved her reaction! Her encouragement after reading the first draft of this book instilled my confidence in the story.

I would like to thank my close friend, Triyas for being the beta reader of this book. Her inputs and suggestions helped me a lot in polishing the script.

I would like to thank Gaurab for being by my side in all ups and downs.

Thanks to all my friends and well-wishers for asking me how the book is shaping up and when it will release.

Thanks to my readers for your love, support and kind words. You have my eternal gratitude. I hope you enjoy reading this book.

I would like to thank Malini Nair for letting me know about the Wordit Art Fund and selecting my manuscript for it.

Big Thanks to the entire team at BecomeShakespeare for their hard work, support and encouragement.

Finally, I would thank God and my Mom for blessing me and showing me the way.

CONTENTS

PROLOGUE

It was an abhorrent sight. Blood swept down from the slit of the wrist, turning the shirt and the sheet of the hospital bed crimson. The nurses yelled out for doctors for attending the patient at 10 pm in the thunderous night.

Akashi took a long sigh to ebb down the jitters running down her spine. She saw her sister, Ipsha lying unconscious on the hospital bed with no doctors to attend her.

"When will a doctor attend my sister?" Akashi asked with trembling lips to the nurse who glanced at her with disgust.

"So, the girl who has slit her wrist is your younger sister. Such a young girl committing suicide! " The nurse blurted out the words rubbing salt in Akashi's fresh wounds.

"Doctor Sharma will be here within some time. Wait." The nurse said after scanning Akashi from top to bottom.

Akashi sat on the wooden bench outside the room where Ipsha has been laid. She said a silent prayer for her sister, who is the only person she has in this vast world. The sound of the thunder interrupted her prayer and made her feel uneasy. Right then, a nurse summoned her, who unlike the previous one had kind eyes and a thin smile.

"Doctor Sharma is attending your sister. He has told you to sit in his cabin as he wants to talk to you about your sister." The nurse said and gave Akashi the directions to Dr. Sharma's cabin.

As every minute ticked past in the clock, Akashi's patience wore off, sitting in the cabin. She remembered the absolute berserk way in which Ipsha behaved before she slit her wrist with the fruit knife. Akashi dug her nails on her skin as she recalled Ipsha's tears and her screams calling out 'Arjun'.

"Hello, this is Dr. Sharma." Akashi's disturbing thoughts

11

got faded by the doctor's voice. She looked at him blankly, fearing to hear the worst.

"It's a fortune that Ipsha is safe now. If the slit was a few centimeters below, it would be perhaps difficult to save her. I have injected her sleeping drug because she needs a deep sleep." The doctor smiled at Akashi after completing his words. Akashi mumbled a meek thank you and covered her face with her hands as she realized she could have lost Ipsha.

"Why did she slit her wrist?" The doctor asked the question which was inevitable yet excruciating.

Akashi looked at the doctor with tear-stained eyes. His kind and affable face calmed her to some extent. She looked through the window and noticed that the rain had stopped and so had the thunder. The sky was quite tranquil; the clock read midnight. The beautiful landscapes of Kalimpong were concealed in the blanket of darkness. Dr. Sharma kept looking at Akashi as she studied her surroundings.

"I know being an elder sister, it hurts to talk about the reason behind your sister's attempt at suicide. But I need to know the reason as I am her doctor. I hope not, but if Ipsha again attempts suicide after regaining her senses, we can't help unless we know what's wrong with her." The doctor explained.

"I don't know where I should begin. Everything seems so strange to me now. I still can't understand why she took such a desperate step." Akashi winced.

"Tell me the entire thing so that I get a clear picture. It's midnight now. My duty is until 6 in the morning. We have enough time." Dr. Sharma proposed.

"Trust me. It's only for Ipsha's well-being." Dr. Sharma said in a convincing tone. Akashi looked through the window with a heavy heart as she realized that she has to share so much about her and Ipsha's life to a stranger. She didn't want the doctor to judge Ipsha or her, but she had no options.

"Don't over think. I assure you that it's only for Ipsha's

treatment and well-being. There is a saying that you should never hide anything from doctors and lawyers. Unless they know the entire truth, they cannot help you." The doctor repeated until Akashi started speaking.

Best Friend

"A sister is like an extension of your own being, whose presence makes you feel complete, sheltered and unruffled."

The shrill noise of utensils falling on the floor disrupted Akashi's sleep. Akashi opened her drowsy eyes and found the blanket of darkness spread all over her room. She never sleeps without switching on the dim light of her room as she has nyctophobia.

Akashi tried to find her cellphone for some source of light when she saw a skull approaching her. Akashi screeched until she saw her mischievous sister's face behind the skeleton mask.

"Hey Sis, it's so effortless to scare you." Ipsha laughed as she switched on the lights and noticed her elder sister's fear packed face.

"It's not funny, Ipsha. I almost had a mini heart attack. What are you doing in my room late at night?" Akashi said, punching Ipsha on her belly to stop her laughter.

"Happy Birthday, Akashi. I just thought to make the start of your birthday a little adventurous. Anyways, here's your surprise." Ipsha gifted Akashi a purple stole on which she had done a beautiful abstract painting.

"Hey, this is so creative. You are so talented, my little sister." Akashi said with moist eyes as she marveled at Ipsha's creation.

"Why have you born so emotional? God could have given some scraps of emotion to me too."

"Then, this house would have turned into a small lake with both of our tears." Akashi said and Ipsha started laughing.

Although Akashi D'Souza and Ipsha D'Souza are extremely different from each other, the two sisters share an inseparable bond. They live in Kalimpong, a picturesque and remote hill station of West Bengal. Today, on the 5th of May, Akashi turned twenty-four. Ipsha is younger to her by seven years. Ipsha currently studies in class twelve in St.Augustine's School, where her father was the principal for more than a decade.

Four years ago, a landslide somewhere between Siliguri and Kalimpong killed their parents. Akashi had taken every responsibility of Ipsha on her own shoulders. From her elder sister, she became Ipsha's mom and dad. They have some supportive neighbors to look after them, but Akashi is too independent to rely on anyone else for support.

After completing her masters in English, Akashi got the job of assistant professor in English at Kalimpong College. It is the same college where she was a student a few years back. Akashi is fair with a small oval-shaped face. She is of medium height and has beautiful waist length hair. Everyone in Kalimpong seems to love her because of her happy and kind demeanor. She is responsible, resolute and has a helpful nature.

Ipsha is a born rebel and is always against the idea of

pleasing everyone. If she likes someone, she is good towards that individual. If she does not like someone, she doesn't even care to say a 'hello'. Only a few people are fond of Ipsha, if compared to Akashi. People adore Akashi and come to her with a list of complaints against Ipsha.

Two days back, a neighbor came to Akashi with the complaint that Ipsha has broken his window pane. When Akashi asked Ipsha, she said, "Mr. Ansari is an old man of fifty years and he stalks my friends and me in Facebook. Can you imagine that?"

"What rubbish? I haven't seen him in your friend list." Akashi knitted her eyebrows.

"My sweet innocent sister, he is on Facebook by the name, Raj Mishra that has the display picture of a random good-looking guy, may be a model. Rohan can hack Facebook accounts and when he hacked that fake account, we got Mr. Ansari's email id. Just think what sort of a pervert he is! He is lucky that my friends and I have only broken his window pane and not his leg." Ipsha said, moving aside the hair strand that fell on her face.

So this is Ipsha, a cute girl with a rebellious disposition. She is lanky, has shoulder-length hair and is over-protective about Akashi. If anyone hurts Akashi, she won't think twice before breaking that person's teeth.

She always keeps a strict eye on Vihaan, the guy Akashi loves, so that he can never hurt Akashi. Akashi's phone rang when Ipsha was explaining her about the birthday party she has organized.

"Hey...you are late." Akashi said after receiving the phone. She looked at the clock which read 12.30 am.

"Sorry Akashi. Happy Birthday! I thought to call you in the morning as you sleep so early, but a second thought made me try your number." Vihaan apologized.

Akashi and Vihaan have studied in the same school and college. Vihaan got a job in Delhi after college and settled down there with his parents. They meet twice a year and Akashi is insecure about their long-distance relationship. This is not because of her sensitive nature, but because of Vihaan's careless and over-friendly attitude. Akashi cannot understand how Vihaan can befriend just anyone. Whether it's his charm or his temperament, everyone seems to love his company. Moreover, he is irresponsible.

"It's alright." Akashi said, a bit sadly.

"Why are you sounding so sad, dear? It's your birthday. Just cheer up!"

"You won't be there with me today and you are telling me to cheer up with such ease."

"So, is this what curbing your beautiful smile on this special day?"

"Whatever. Who cares! You tell me, how is life in Delhi?"

"I care, Akashi for that beautiful smile on your angelic face."

"Good joke."

"It is not. Just open the door of your house." Vihaan said, surprising Akashi. .

"Oh my God!" Akashi screamed as she comprehended his words.

Akashi rushed to the main door and opened it to find Vihaan standing outside with a bouquet of red roses in his hand. Akashi squealed in delight and ran to Vihaan's arms.

"Oh Akashi, let me in. It's freezing outside." Vihaan said as Akashi embraced him tightly.

"It's great that you have planned this surprise for Akashi, Vihaan. Else if you would have given my innocent sister some excuse, I would have organized your break-up party in Delhi." Ipsha said with a grin.

"How can I miss this chance of partying with the two most beautiful girls in this world? Miss World and Miss Universe." Vihaan winked and wrapped his arms around the two sisters.

17

"Thanks Vihaan for this lovely surprise. I love you." Akashi said, gazing lovingly at Vihaan's face.

"I love you too, sweetheart. I reached Kalimpong in the morning today, but wanted to surprise you in this midnight hour."

"Ha! Midnight hour. Thirty minutes late you were." Ipsha corrected.

"Yeah, punctuality has issues with me from the moment I landed on this earth. I am trying though." Vihaan laughed.

"It's fine, Vihaan. You took the pain of surprising me on my birthday and that means the world to me." Akashi said.

"So I will catch you both in the morning again. Love you gorgeous! Happy Birthday once again!" Vihaan gave a peck on Akashi's lips.

Akashi cuddled Ipsha in exhilaration after Vihaan left.

"You did all these, right?" Akashi asked Ipsha.

"See, I just told Vihaan that either you come to Kalimpong on Akashi's birthday or don't contact her at all. Stay with your happening life in Delhi and let us live in peace here." Ipsha said in one breath.

"That was really rude, Ipsha. Tell me you haven't used these words."

"Chill sister. It's fair. I know Vihaan since I was a child. I have this right on him."

"That you have!" Akashi said with a smile.

"Listen, I have a great idea. Let's kidnap Vihaan so that he can never go back to Delhi, what say?" Ipsha looked at Akashi with twinkling eyes.

"Ipsha, I haven't been bitten by a mad dog yet to be a part of your brilliant idea." Akashi laughed and Ipsha threw a pillow at her. The sisters indulged in a pillow fight and giggled until their belly started aching. They slept together after their belly-laugh, cuddling each other. Sisters are best friends for a lifetime.

HIM

"Sometimes, it is wise to let people go without any complaints. If they are a part of our destiny, they will return after a couple of seasons. Till then, let them dwell in the pages of our memories."

Vihaan was the host in Akashi's birthday party. He wanted Ipsha and Akashi to relax and enjoy without bothering about the guests. The guests comprised Akashi and Ipsha's friends and some nosy neighbors. .

Vihaan gifted Akashi a synthesizer as he knew that the old synthesizer, which belonged to Akashi's mother hardly produced any melody. It was too old to repair, but it stayed in their house as a symbol of their mother. As Akashi played some jazz on the synthesizer, Vihaan looked at her with love and admiration.

Vihaan knew from the beginning that Akashi is a magical girl and that no other girl can ever replace Akashi in his heart. He is firm in his earlier belief, even now, but after he settled in Delhi, he started feeling the dissimilarities between Akashi and him. He felt that Akashi is too good a person for

19

him. He started feeling guilty that his carefree attitude towards life torments Akashi. That's what Ipsha has been telling to him over the phone for the last few months. Vihaan doesn't want to be Akashi's tormentor.

He understands that he fails to fulfill Akashi's expectations every time. He knows that he is forgetful and irresponsible. His attitude towards life and relationships is quite happy-go-lucky, whereas Akashi wants sincerity. As he looked at Akashi's serene face with a burdensome heart, he knew that he has taken the right decision.

While the guests were drowned in Akashi's music, Ipsha's eyes fell on a huge bouquet of orchids at the corner of the room. She had an intuition and moved towards the bouquet. She found a card on it which had her name mentioned. She held the bouquet in her hand and read the card with crooked eyebrows.

Do you know what Ipsha means? It means wish. Yes, dear, you are my one and only wish!

Ipsha crumpled the card after reading the words twice. She threw it from the window out of anger with a palpitating heart. It has been three days since she is getting these anonymous love notes. It was fine when she got such notes at school as it enhanced her popularity and also gave something to gossip with her friends during lunch break.

Getting such a note with flowers at her home was no little joke to laugh about. It implied that the stranger who had been stalking her since the last few days knew her address too. Ipsha winced with fear as she figured out the scenario. She looked outside the window and shivered imagining some stranger, keeping his eyes transfixed on her every move. She drew the curtains impulsively and returned to the vacant seat beside Vihaan.

Ipsha waited for the party to end so that she can share it with Akashi. Whatever was happening during school hours, she treated it as a joke. Now, she was petrified and wanted

Akashi's advice on the matter.

The party ended soon, but Vihaan stayed back as he needed to talk to Akashi on an important matter before leaving for Delhi the next morning. Ipsha wanted to be an audience too, but Vihaan pleaded Ipsha to allow him to talk to Akashi in private.

"Actually, I know what you want to talk to me about. That it's not working and it won't work anymore." Akashi said with a pale face, which made Vihaan feel guilty.

"I am not the right person for you, Akashi. I am forgetful, irresponsible and careless. I am not worthy of being your boyfriend. I forget to call you some days, not because I love you less, but because I am such a careless person. My nature won't change and sticking to me will make you suffer every single day. You cannot accept my careless nature and I cannot match your expectations. It won't work Akashi." Vihaan said these words without looking at Akashi. When he looked at her, he could see innumerable tears which she was fighting her best to hold back.

"I was talking about my mother's old synthesizer…that it's not working and it won't work anymore." Akashi said amidst her sobs which made Vihaan realize the mess that he had caused.

Vihaan pulled Akashi to his chest. He kissed her forehead and started speaking, "Please Akashi, I don't want you to cry every day for me. I will always be with you whenever you need me. That's a promise because I love you and no other girl can ever take the space that you have in my heart. But I can't be your boyfriend. I am too careless and I will keep dragging our relationship to the gutter. Ipsha is right, I torment you too much. You don't deserve this. You deserve only happiness."

"Why on earth are you like this? You only love yourself and no one else, Vihaan." Akashi said, moving away from Vihaan.

"I know. This is why it is better we break up."

"Just leave. I don't want you in my life, anymore." Akashi said, her breathing heavy with anger, humiliation and sorrow. Vihaan left the house, without any word.

Ipsha heard the entire conversation from the other side of the wall and felt miserable that she could not save Akashi from this agony. Ipsha knew that Vihaan was careless, but she thought that Vihaan loved Akashi too much to let her go.

One part of Ipsha wanted to punch Vihaan on his face and break his teeth for the pain he inflicted on her elder sister. But another part of her was thankful to Vihaan for taking this decision. She was well aware of the countless nights when Akashi could not sleep because she had not heard from Vihaan the entire day.

Akashi expected a lot from Vihaan while Vihaan was too busy to live his life to the fullest. Such a carefree guy is never a suitable match for Akashi, Ipsha knew that. Ipsha went inside her sister's room and sat beside Akashi, who was sobbing incessantly. As Ipsha kept her palm on Akashi's hand, Akashi started crying louder.

"I love you, Ipsha. Promise me that you won't leave me ever." Akashi said.

"He left you for your good, Akashi. Just remember, he was meant to be a part of your memory, not a part of your destiny." Ipsha said and embraced Akashi.

Although Ipsha wanted to talk to Akashi about those anonymous love notes, she deferred the subject until the next evening. In the darkness of the night, Akashi lamented about Vihaan and Ipsha thought about the uncanny stranger and his creepy love notes for her. When she got the first note on her desk after the lunch break, she thought it to be a classmate of hers who had developed a crush on her. The first note read:

Every day I come here, just to catch a glimpse of you. You are more beautiful than the town of Kalimpong.

Ipsha bullied every boy in her class to find out who had dared to send her that creepy love note but to no avail. When she found the second love note on the road while she was returning home, she understood that none of her classmates had sent her the previous note.

I learned that your name is Ipsha. Guess what, I am uttering and writing your name countless times, since the moment I learned it.

Ipsha was shocked that a stranger took the pain of learning her name and kept on uttering it as if it is a song. The girls told her that they envied her and the boys made her feel like a star. At the core of her heart, Ipsha did not exactly hate it. The next day on the morning of Akashi's birthday, Ipsha got another note which was longer than the earlier ones.

I know it's lame, but I am sure that I have fallen in love with you Ipsha. I can't think of anything else except your smile and voice. Oh yes, I have heard you talking to your friends and I have countless pictures of yours in my camera.

Ipsha was bewildered to know that her stalker had clicked her pictures too. She became hysterical when she read the note, but her friends pacified her saying that it might be a joke. When Ipsha got the bouquet of orchids and the fourth note in the evening of Akashi's birthday, she understood that the stranger knew her address too.

She was also sure about the countless pictures that her stalker had clicked without her knowledge. Ipsha grew anxious with every passing minute and she could not let even a dash of sleep settle in her eyes. It was morning within a blink; the fastest morning she has ever witnessed.

THE OBSESSIVE TUNE

"The mind is a crazy little thing, always keen to invite some danger. It often thinks the unthinkable, wants the unattainable and knocks on the forbidden door when the other door is open."

Ipsha looked at the English teacher's face who was explaining Act 3 of George Bernard Shaw's Pygmalion. The teacher smiled at Ipsha, thinking that Ipsha was paying attention to her lecture instead of gossiping with her friends.

It is incredible how the countenance of a human being can be so deceiving. Who can say that beneath the attentive and placid face of Ipsha, a turbulent tempest is taking place? Not even a word of what the teacher was explaining made way to Ipsha's ears. She only remembered Akashi's relentless tears. Although she is the younger sister, Ipsha has always been protective of Akashi. She cannot endure Akashi's tears and when Akashi is sad, she gets trapped in an invisible cage of melancholy.

"Ipsha, tell us what would you have done if you were in Eliza Doolittle's place? Would you keep quiet when you are

24

not acknowledged for your efforts or would you react as hysterically as Eliza did in this Act?" The teacher asked, meddling Ipsha's train of thoughts.

Ipsha stood up, clueless to what the question meant. She had hardly heard a word to comprehend what she would have done if she was in Eliza's place. She cleared her throat and said, "Ma'am, I am disturbed. I did not pay attention to the class."

The teacher neared Ipsha and said in an authoritarian tone, "I know that, Ipsha. You cannot fool me by looking at me. I could well understand that your mind was in some other place."

As the teacher mouthed these words, the entire class started coughing and smiling, to Ipsha's disbelief. The lunch break bell rang and Ipsha felt somewhat relieved.

"I know this is an age to get diverted from studies to romantic flights of fancy, but my class is not made for your reveries. So, from next time, if you can't pay attention to my class, you are free to stay outside." The teacher said and left the class.

"Ipsha's mind is with her lovelorn stalker." The guys sang, making Ipsha turn red in anger. She regretted for letting her classmates know about the stalker.

"You people are sick. I have other issues in life to think about." Ipsha said and left the class.

Ipsha's best friend, Sandra followed her to the corridor.

"Why did you overreact like that?" Sandra asked, offering a cheese sandwich to Ipsha. Ipsha took the sandwich and told Sandra that she was upset because of Akashi's breakup. She thinks she is responsible for the breakup as she told Vihaan countless times how his careless attitude tormented Akashi.

"You did the right thing. And I was thinking all the while, you were absent-minded because of that stalker. When you told me yesterday that he knows your address, my heart was pounding in fear. It is no little joke, Ipsha. He seems to be a dangerous person. You must talk to your elder sister immediately about it." Sandra suggested.

A teacher called Sandra for carrying the notebooks to the staff room. Sandra stuffed the lunch-box in Ipsha's hand and went unwillingly.

As Ipsha munched a sandwich, a beautiful tune reached her ears. It was a tune which she has never heard. She was sure that it was not a tune of a song from any movie or album. However, the tune had a magnetic melody which made her smile. She seemed to enjoy the tune which was playing again and again.

"Wow! So we have a new musician in Kalimpong who plays a mouth organ in the streets of the town and cheer people around." Ipsha said delightfully to herself. She immersed herself in the melody of the tune and didn't realize when it stopped.

"Hey, why are you smiling?" Sandra asked.

"That tune...someone was playing the harmonica." Ipsha said.

"Really? I didn't hear."

"You were in the staff room, Sandra."

"Right. Who was it, playing a mouth organ in the streets of Kalimpong like the Pied Piper of Hamlin?" Sandra laughed.

"How will I know, Sandra? I was enjoying the tune from here. I wish it never stopped." Ipsha said, closing her eyes.

The classes started again and Ipsha decided to be a little more attentive. Her plans were unfruitful as she kept thinking about the tune which she heard during the lunch break. The same melody which filled Ipsha with euphoria a few minutes back disturbed her then. It was because of her intuition.

What if this is the stalker man?

Ipsha shuddered at the thought and couldn't pay attention

to any of the classes. She pushed her intuition aside by presuming that she needs a long sleep. As school got over, Ipsha headed straight towards her home without gossiping with her friends.

"Ipsha, wait for a while." Sandra beckoned.

"Sandra, I am weary. I will call you later at night." Ipsha said.

Ipsha's school is fifteen minutes walking distance from her house. The streets of Kalimpong were quite secluded in the evening. The white orchids blooming on one side of the road alleviated Ipsha's tiredness. Ipsha has always loved orchids more than any other flower. This is because Kalimpong is an abode of orchids. You can find orchids of various colors and designs in every alley and lane of Kalimpong.

The soothing breeze of the hills touched Ipsha's skin. She looked at the beautiful sky, which was a riot of colors as the sun prepared to bid adieu to the mountains. Being born and brought up in the lap of Nature, Ipsha has always found Nature to be her healer. She wonders how people who live in cities survive without the healing touch of Nature.

As Ipsha admired the beauty of Nature, the same tune startled her again. The tune was more vivid this time and she looked around to locate the source of the tune. She walked towards the direction from where the music was coming until she was stopped by a little girl. Ipsha smiled at the girl when she handed her a piece of paper. Ipsha realized that the note was from the stalker. She heaved a sigh and started reading.

I know you are in love with this tune, ain't you? Yes Ipsha, it's me. You guessed it right. I knew you would understand that it's your crazy lover calling you through a tune.

Ipsha's pulsating heartbeats made her shiver as she finished reading the note. The little girl was nowhere, but the tune persisted. It was a tune of obsession and longing. Ipsha could no longer hold her composure and she ran towards the direction from where the music was coming. The tune teased her as she couldn't locate its source.

A wave of frustration washed over her as she followed the tune. She felt exhausted after a while and gave up her search, holding her knees. She looked completely frazzled and messy.

As she stood straight, she saw a silhouette in the distance. It was the silhouette of a tall man who had a cowboy hat on his head. Ipsha could decipher that she has found the source of the obsessive tune. It was the time of sundown and Ipsha had difficulty in observing the person. She walked in the direction of the silhouette with her aching legs.

The purple sky, the haunting tune and the attractive silhouette did some magic to Ipsha. A strong yearning to see the man who has been stalking her for a week grew in her heart. She followed the silhouette, but it disappeared in the darkness. The tune also faded gradually, disappointing and frustrating her.

Who are you? Is there no way to reach out to you? Stop making me crazy.

Ipsha mumbled the words looking at the darkness, but the silhouette could no longer be seen. She couldn't fathom why the person, claiming to love her, does not appear in front of her. She wanted to see the person who is incredibly crazy for her. On second thoughts, she questioned her decision.

Do I really want to see him?

A bizarre combination of fear and desire grasped her. There was definitely that lingering fear in Ipsha's mind about the stalker, but now, there was also a delirious desire of seeing the person. It was an erratic feeling, something that Ipsha couldn't put into words. She tried to hush her turbulent mind and finally walked towards home.

HIS HAUNTING SILHOUETTE

"There are some moments in life when we can feel countless emotions somersaulting within us. One emotion follows the other, just like the sky that changes color swiftly during dawn and dusk."

Ipsha was quivering when she reached home. Their house help, Malati Masi opened the door and was shocked to see Ipsha in that condition.

"Please give me a glass of water, Masi." Ipsha pleaded.

Malati Masi was on leave as she went to Kolkata for her daughter's childbirth. She returned today and was disheartened to hear about Akashi's breakup. Malati Masi has been working in their house since Akashi was a newborn baby. She is more like a family member and less like a house help. Akashi trusts and confides in her.

Earlier, she used to go back to her house after the day's work. But after Akashi and Ipsha's parents died in the accident, she decided to stay in their house so that she can look after the two sisters. She has a grown up son who stays in Kalimpong with his family and a daughter who is married

29

in Kolkata. She loves the two sisters like her own children.

Ipsha threw her school bag on the sofa and grabbed the glass of water that Malati Masi brought for her. She got hiccups as she tried to gulp the water all at once.

"Drink slowly, Ipsha. Are you feeling sick?" Malati Masi asked with motherly concern.

"I will be fine, Masi. Good to see you, after long." Ipsha smiled at the caring woman, who smiled in return.

"Ipsha, what made you reach home so late? I was almost dying of tension." Akashi walked in the living room.

Ipsha tried to speak, but her hiccups interrupted her.

"Here, have some more water." Akashi moved the water bottle to Ipsha's side. Ipsha wolfed down the entire water in the bottle and sat on the sofa, exhausted.

"I called Sandra just ten minutes back and she said that you left school much earlier today. Then, what made you get so late?" Akashi continued, much to Ipsha's annoyance.

Ipsha had decided to tell Akashi about the stalker in the morning, but right then, she changed her mind. The reason behind hiding about the stalker was unknown to her. Perhaps, she did not have the right words to frame the entire situation and present it in front of Akashi. Moreover, she knew how emotional and apprehensive Akashi can get. This incident would probably drive away Akashi's sleep at nights.

"A little girl lost her way. I was just helping her out and so, got late." Ipsha blurted out the lie quite confidently.

Akashi sat on the sofa and embraced Ipsha.

"You are the only person I have in this world, dear. I get worried about you too much. I am sorry if I have been a little bossy. I know I have promised you that I will be your friend always." Akashi said holding Ipsha's hand.

Ipsha hugged her and assured that she has complete right to scold her, without feeling guilty.

"You are my Mom, Dad as well as my elder sister. Don't apologize, Akashi." Ipsha said.

As Ipsha moved to her room to freshen up, Akashi again became a prisoner of past memories. Despite her wish, the dusk brought along thoughts of Vihaan to her arid heart. Akashi felt a frantic urge to call Vihaan, but she remembered what their parting words were. Vihaan went away when Akashi told him that she doesn't want him in her life anymore. He did not even give a last try; he did not even say anything against it.

She deleted Vihaan's number from her phone, although she knew his number by heart.

No matter how unconditional or selfless your love is, you should never beg for the other person's love in return. This is the most brutal thing that you can do to yourself and to the love that you have in your heart. Akashi knew she still loved Vihaan, but she decided that she won't beg for his love and attention.

It is unfortunate that Vihaan could never feel the depth of Akashi's love for him. May be, he loved himself too much to feel someone else's love. Or perhaps, he loved his happy-go-lucky life more than anybody. The responsibility of a relationship was too much for him.

Akashi decided to keep all the physical evidences that can remind her of Vihaan away from her sight. She was sure that it would provide her with some tranquility.

**

Ipsha was lost in her thoughts even during dinner. When Akashi asked her, she said that she was thinking about a painting that she started working on after returning from school.

"That's wonderful, Ipsha. I would love to see the painting that you are working on." Akashi said with a smile.

"Did Vihaan call you today?" Ipsha asked.

"Why will he call me?" Akashi said, lowering her gaze.

"To apologize for last night" Ipsha said, fiddling with her fork.

"I am fine, darling. You don't worry so much. I am really fine." Akashi said, trying to smile.

"I hope you become fine soon. I can't see you in such a miserable state." Ipsha said, looking at her sister.

"I promise I am trying." Akashi muttered, more to herself.

Ipsha nodded but was unsure if Akashi could forget Vihaan so easily. Akashi's eyes did not support her words at all.

"Okay now, leave this tiresome topic of Vihaan. Don't forget to show me your latest artwork after dinner." Akashi said with eagerness.

Unlike the other times, Ipsha was not so keen to show her canvas to Akashi. She brought Akashi to her room reluctantly after dinner. The painting was not yet complete, but the drawing could be deciphered. It was the silhouette of a man with a large hat and a harmonica-like substance in his hand. The backdrop of the painting was the woods of Kalimpong. The man was walking in the woods of Kalimpong after dusk has set in. Ipsha had not yet used colors on it.

"Beautiful! A mysterious, eerie feeling emanates from this painting. Any person, who would take a look at this painting, would get that feel almost immediately." Akashi said, admiring her sister's talent.

"I have not used colors on it yet. You are praising me too much." Ipsha said with modesty.

"No! You know I can be a harsh critic. But, this is pure genius. Name this painting: *His haunting silhouette*. This will sell in a moment if you conduct an exhibition of your paintings; watch my words." Akashi said.

Ipsha smiled and gazed at her canvas. The name of the painting given by Akashi reverberated in her ears: *His haunting silhouette*.

"How do such brilliant ideas pop into your mind? From

where did you get the idea of this painting?" Akashi asked.

The question made Ipsha feel uneasy.

"I don't know. Just…like…that!" Ipsha said with a little struggle.

"Genius you are! Go to sleep early. Tomorrow you have school." Akashi gave a peck on Ipsha's cheek and walked towards her room.

Ipsha felt relieved. Akashi's interrogation was making her feel awkward and uncomfortable. She started working on her painting again as thoughts of the man grasped her. *If only I could see him once! Just once!*

Ipsha did not know why she was craving to see the man who had given her so much stress and tension all these days. She did not know why she wanted to keep him as a secret from everyone, including Akashi and Sandra. She promised Sandra that she would call her at night, but she did not feel like calling her.

She enjoyed being alone with her thoughts. She had a mystifying desire of knowing the man who claimed to be her crazy lover. The tune of harmonica and his silhouette played with her senses.

After an hour or two, she was almost done with the painting. She looked at her creation with contentment and ecstasy. After a long time, she felt so happy after working on a painting. Right at that moment, a sound gave her cold feet.

Isn't this the same tune that I have heard during the day at my school and in the evening while returning home? Oh, my God…yes it is!

Ipsha was appalled beyond words. She looked at the window beside her bed which had the curtains moved aside. The pitch-black darkness outside and the tune which sounded quite clear made her tongue-tied. Her breathing became heavier as the tune made way to her ears and settled deep down the corners of her mind. She looked at the clock which read midnight.

Gathering some amount of courage, she crawled towards

the window. She took a torch and focused it outside. The tune had stopped by then. Ipsha moved the torch to every nook and corner outside, but couldn't see anyone or anything. As she was about to switch off the torch light, she heard the rustling of leaves from a particular direction. She figured out the direction from where the sound came and then in a flash, she focused the torch light in that direction. Finally, she could see what her eyes hankered for. Although for just a few seconds, but she could see the familiar silhouette of the man going away.

Ipsha shut the windows at once. She inhaled and exhaled deeply in nervousness. Sweat beads covered her forehead. The silhouette of the hat-man and the melodious tune seemed to haunt her obsessively. She felt that she was possessed by this man whom she has never seen, but she could feel his presence always.

Am I crazy? Despite feeling scared of this person who is stalking me at midnight outside my house, I am so desperate to see him once.

Ipsha couldn't understand why she was feeling this way for the person whose name, face and identity were unknown to her. He has seen her and knows quite a lot about her, but she doesn't know anything. Yet, she felt a strange magnetic pull towards this person. She was scared, but she wanted to see the face of her fear.

Her new painting was faintly visible in the dim light of her room. She kept gazing at the painting and thought about the stalker. Her mind drew hundreds of faces that could go with such an attractive contour. She was quite confident that this man is handsome. Her thoughts heightened her desires. Although it was an outlandish feeling, Ipsha enjoyed the desire and fantasy that were lurking in the lap of her fear.

THE ARDENT CRAVING

"A person's desire has no bounds. It is wild and difficult to be caged. It starts as a tiny seed and then grows exponentially into a mammoth tree with innumerable branches."

So, my Ipsha is an artist. And she has captured me on her canvas. Wow! I have definitely fallen for you more after seeing your painting.

How I wish it was your heart where you captured me instead of your canvas!

Ipsha got the note from the stalker after her school ended that day. Ipsha was thinking during the classes why he has been silent the entire day. She couldn't hear the tune and she also didn't receive any note from him during the school hours. She was somewhat upset as she did not want this crazy thing to end and, fortunately, it did not end.

She was returning home with Sandra that day. After Sandra entered her house, Ipsha got a note from a passerby who said that the man standing there has sent it to her. When she looked at the mentioned direction, she couldn't see anyone. This has been a regular ritual now, which no longer terrified Ipsha. She still wondered what her lover gained by watching her from a distance and by not showing his face.

As Ipsha read the note, an idea popped into her mind.

"This hide and seek game should be over." Ipsha muttered as she took out a pen from her bag.

She saw that the back side of the love note was empty. Without wasting a minute, she started scribbling on it:

Enough of this hide and seek game! If you really love me, then what is stopping you from directly talking to me?

Ipsha left the note on the road and started walking. She was sure that her lover was keeping an eye on her every move. So, she was confident that after she walks away, he would definitely pick the note from the road and read it.

Ipsha thought that if Sandra would have been with her, she would have never allowed her to write back to the stalker. She remembered Sandra's words, "You are getting frenetic day by day, Ipsha. Why haven't you told to your sister that the stalker was stalking you at midnight outside your house?"

Ipsha moved aside Sandra's thoughts from her mind and waited for the reply of her message. She was exhilarated when she found a piece of paper at the turn of a road. After collecting her composure, she quietly opened the note and started reading it.

Today, I am convinced that you have fallen in love with me. And that also, without seeing me ever! I know that you can feel my presence around you, always and you are craving to meet me. Well, the other name of love is patience. So, my dearest Ipsha, wait for some time!

Ipsha frowned as she read the note. She was desperate to meet this man and he was playing games with her. She felt dejected as her plan did not bear fruits. She thought that the man would at least drop his number or tell her a place where she could meet him. But here, what she received was another game. Ipsha decided that she would no more entertain this mad person. She made up her mind to ignore all his love notes and lunatic gestures as she headed towards home.

The ambiance of her home was gloomy. Ever since Akashi and Vihaan broke up, it seems that she is staying at her home alone. Akashi hardly watches television or listens to music these days. She doesn't even play the synthesizer or hum a song. It is only during the dinner time when she talks to Ipsha about how their days went. Apart from that, Akashi stays in her room. She has embraced solitude.

Ipsha wants her to be normal and chirpy, but she can fathom what Akashi is going through. Vihaan was her emotional anchor or at least Akashi perceived him to be her anchor. Ipsha always felt that Vihaan was irresponsible and so there would be hardly any difference if Vihaan did not stay in Akashi's life. But she was wrong.

Sleep eluded Ipsha that night and her sobs echoed in her room. Although Ipsha bears a hard exterior, she is delicate from inside. She felt tired, physically and mentally. She missed the time when Akashi and she used to talk non-stop for hours and watched movies together. She missed her Mom and Dad. Pangs of loneliness gripped her tight and she had no one to share her feelings with.

She thought about the lunatic stalker and cried some more, thinking what made her desperate enough to write back to him. She hated her life at that moment and thought how peaceful and happy her friends are. She envied Sandra for the perfect family she had. She envied Rohan for having a sweet girlfriend to share things with. Ipsha started envying almost everyone she knew in her life and wallowed in self-pity.

Ipsha's sobs became uncontrollable with the wave of pain crashing against her heart. The waves kept hitting the shore of her heart, again and again, pulling her into the melancholic sea which she tried her best to escape.

She wanted to break down totally. She thought if only her parents were alive today, Akashi and she would have got a perfect life. Life wouldn't have been a merciless struggle, every single day.

The only way Ipsha knew to have control on her mind was to draw and paint. So, she took out a fresh paper and started drawing. She tried to draw a vulnerable girl, sheathed with fear and anxiety.

When she was in the middle of the sketch, her phone rang. She looked at the clock and wondered who can call her at 1 am in the morning. With slight apprehension, she answered the call.

"Ipsha..." The voice on the other side of the phone called out her name. It was a man's voice and undoubtedly, it was the most attractive voice that she had ever heard. She was silent when the voice called out her name again.

"Dearest Ipsha...are you hearing?"

On hearing *Dearest Ipsha,* she was confident that this was her crazy stalker.

"Yes. Who is it?" Ipsha finally asked with pulsating heartbeats.

"I think you can guess who I am. Right?" The man said after laughing for a few seconds. His voice enthralled Ipsha.

"I guess you are the person who has been stalking me for more than a week." Ipsha said, mustering a little courage.

"Yes, my love."

Ipsha blushed when the voice on the other side of the phone said *my love.* No has ever called her *love.*

"But...I don't know anything about you...not even your name." Ipsha continued, confidence returning back to her voice.

"And you want to know everything about me starting from my name and profession to how I look."

"Yes. I do. And I think that's fair on my part. You know everything about me and I don't know anything. This is unfair. Don't you agree?" Ipsha said with a smile. She was surprised how she could talk to the stranger so comfortably.

The man laughed at Ipsha's words. He found her words amusing. Ipsha was taken aback.

"Hey...say something." Ipsha insisted.

"Arjun."

"Eh...what?"

"My name, sweetheart. It's Arjun Walia."

Ipsha was exhilarated on learning her stalker's name.

"Arjun." She repeated his name.

"Wow! My name sounds different in your voice. Say it again, one more time." Arjun said.

"Arjun...I want to meet you." Ipsha said.

"Your wish is my command. But you have to wait for the perfect time."

"Okay. I will wait."

"I love you." Arjun said, making Ipsha speechless.

"You haven't even met me once."

"But I know each and every thing about you. And one more thing, I also know that you are falling in love with me." Arjun said with confidence.

"You are crazy." Ipsha said with a huge grin.

"Just for you! Go to sleep now. I promise we will meet soon."

"Goodnight." Ipsha was sad that the call ended.

"And your voice is as sweet as your face. Goodnight." Arjun said and disconnected the call.

"And your voice is sexy." Ipsha said, gazing at her phone.

All her sadness and anxiety seemed to disappear into nothingness by the time the call ended. Arjun was not wrong in perceiving her. Although she wasn't sure if she was falling in love with him, she was sure that she longed for him. She wanted to see how he looks and wanted to ask him why he loves her. She wanted to know when he had seen her for the first time and what made him so crazy for her. Arjun's voice and silhouette have already given her subtle hints about how attractive he is.

She looked at the mirror and studied her features. She is tall and slim with medium-length wavy hair. Her complexion is milk-white and her eyes are dark brown in color. She has a small nose and full lips. She feels that she looks average, not cute or pretty. There are prettier girls in her school and in her class too. Out of Akashi and Ipsha, it's always Akashi who bags a thousand compliments about her beauty. People look at Ipsha and say how lanky she is.

Ipsha contemplated about what could have made Arjun fall in love with her. Unable to find a suitable answer to her question, she decided to sleep as she had school the next day. She felt relaxed, but the ardent craving for Arjun didn't escape her mind.

THE LONG WAIT

"Waiting is painful, testing and arduous. It makes us restless, but finally, when it rains after months of blazing heat, the feeling is too miraculous to capture in words."

Ipsha sighed as Akashi's voice disrupted her sleep. She wanted to sleep some more. Arjun's hypnotic voice and their first conversation greeted her mind as she tossed and turned on the bed. A large smile formed on her face as she thought of Arjun.

"Ipsha! Are you smiling in your dreams?" Akashi's voice brought Ipsha back to reality. She opened her eyes in a jiffy.

"I have been trying to wake you up since the last two hours, but you kept on sleeping. So I thought it wouldn't be too big an issue if you miss school one day. And today is Friday. So, you will have straight three-day holidays." Akashi said with a smile. She looked pretty in an orange *kurti* and jeans. The vanilla body mist went along well with her soothing persona. Ipsha realized that Akashi was ready for her college.

41

She smiled at Akashi, but her face turned pale as she looked at the clock which read 9am. Her school has already started and nothing could be done. She wondered if her alarm did not wake her up in time or she had switched it off in drowsiness. Ipsha was visibly upset.

"There is nothing to be upset, my dear. You watch TV and enjoy yourself. Breakfast is on the table. Tell Malati Masi what you want to have for lunch. She will make it. I am leaving now otherwise I will be late." Akashi kissed Ipsha's forehead and left the house with a smile.

Ipsha followed Akashi to close the door. She wondered if Arjun would be waiting for her in front of her school. The thought made her restless and fidgety. As she had her breakfast, an idea struck her mind.

She picked her phone and dialed the last number which called her. Her enthusiasm was blown to ashes within a minute as the number was switched off. Presuming that Arjun sleeps with his mobile switched off, she kept trying the number in periodic intervals. She couldn't concentrate on watching television or listening to music. She only wanted to talk to Arjun and ask him when they would be meeting. Her desperation multiplied in leaps and bounds.

Finally, when Ipsha dialed the number after having her lunch, she could hear it ringing. She waited to hear Arjun's voice with bated breath, but was once again met with sheer disappointment. A male voice answered the call, but she was sure it was not Arjun. This voice was soft, unlike Arjun's baritone voice. Ipsha heaved a long sigh and thought that it must be a friend of Arjun. She calmed herself, but on asking about Arjun, she got a shocking reply that no one named Arjun is available at this number. The person on the other side of the phone disconnected the line, leaving her thwarted.

Ipsha cupped her face as she thought about Arjun. She hated him for teasing her every time and leaving her with this vulnerable longing. She always knew this person was not good for her, but still, she couldn't get away from his thoughts.

Despite planning to tell Akashi about him, she stopped herself every time. The fervency of this secret affair was making her crazy. She thought that she has finally solved the riddle of the stalker, but now, she is stuck with yet another brain-teaser. *The riddle called Arjun!*

Ipsha tried to calm herself by focusing on her first love: painting. She decided that she won't let anything or anyone come between her and her painting. Her brushes and paints could successfully keep her diverted for some time until the green paint was all used up, adding up to her frustration. Since the painting on which Ipsha was working needed green color, she got angry. As she touched the other paint tubes, she realized that she needed to buy a box of paint so that her painting won't be interrupted soon.

Ipsha gets angry if she is interrupted in the middle of her painting. Even Akashi doesn't talk to Ipsha when she is busy with her canvas. The world of canvas and colors provide a beautiful refuge where she can escape from every ounce of pain, distress and angst.

Ipsha made up her mind to walk to the nearby market to buy a new box of paint and new brushes. She did not have anything interesting to do at home till Akashi returns in the evening and there was also no great weekend plans. She thought that indulging in her passion is the best possible way to stay engaged and happy. Moreover, she knew that Arjun's thoughts would haunt her if she sits idle.

Ipsha wore a red tee and a denim Capri. After running the comb once on her wavy hair and dabbing a slight lip gloss, she was ready. She told Malati Masi that she would be back within an hour from the market. As she went outside, she saw that the weather was pleasant and the sky looked beautiful.

"Summers in hill stations are lovely." Ipsha heard a

tourist speaking to her husband. She wondered how the summers in cities were. She did not have any idea. Although her mother was from Kolkata, she does not have any fond memories of the city. Akashi often tells that they have all visited Kolkata once during Durga Puja, but Ipsha was only four years old then.

Ipsha's mind wavered to the places beyond Kalimpong. She realized that her horizon has been so narrow and restricted. She is a mountain girl who has only been to the neighboring hill stations such as Kurseong and Darjeeling; the furthest she has ever been to is Sikkim. The seventeen years of her life have been spent completely within hills and in solitude. The hustle bustle of cities is only a figment of imagination for her that has been shaped from watching television and reading books.

Akashi was lucky in this regard. She has gone for both her school and college excursions out of Kalimpong. She has been to Mumbai and Puri. She also has memories of Kolkata. So, she knows it all: the lifestyle of cities, the beauty of beaches and different kinds of people. Ipsha, on the other hand, is naïve and ignorant of the world beyond the beautiful, majestic hills. Ipsha felt pity for her limited horizon, but thinking it to be her destiny, she tried to shrug off the thought over her shoulders.

Ipsha bought the required materials from a stationery shop and walked towards home. A tinge of loneliness clouded her heart as she contemplated about the several voids that existed in her life. She decided to take the isolated, shortcut route towards her house. The people around, in their beaming and delightful demeanor, made her melancholic.

As Ipsha walked, weary with the burden of her thoughts, something stopped her. She felt someone is following her. She turned back and found no one around. Disregarding it as her hallucination, she walked with quick steps until she got that eerie feeling again, this time more clearly. She again turned back and looked around with slight trepidation.

She remembered the several stories about ghosts that dwell in the forests of Kalimpong. Her fear made her recall those stories that she had heard umpteen times in her childhood. She regretted her idea of choosing this isolated route. Suddenly, she heard a magical tune.

Yes! It's the tune of Arjun's harmonica.

An ecstatic smile appeared on her face immediately as she realized that Arjun is nearby and it must be Arjun who was following her all this while. Ipsha decided to follow the tune to reach Arjun, but something made her change her mind, right away.

He is playing the same provoking games with me. I won't give in to his whims, this time. I won't.

Ipsha tried to divert her mind from the melodious and haunting tune that possessed her soul. She walked hurriedly, but the sound of the mellifluous tune was still persistent in the air. After a lot of self-constraint, Ipsha felt completely powerless. With every passing second, the tune seemed to provoke her even more. Finally, shedding her hesitation, Ipsha decided the follow the tune. She could understand that the tune was approaching from her right side. Although it was the opposite direction of her house, she decided to approach the source of the tune.

Ipsha walked in the right direction, but as she approached closer to the tune, the tune moved far away. She could understand that the person playing the tune is walking away from her as she approached him. Ipsha started running towards the direction of the tune until she could finally see the hat-man, Arjun. And this was the first time she could actually see him and not his silhouette, albeit from a far away distance.

From the back, Arjun looked extremely tall. He wore a black jacket, black jeans and a brown hat. As Ipsha observed

45

Arjun, she was completely captivated in his thoughts, so much that she lost him.

Ipsha sulked as she lost Arjun yet again. Without giving up, she followed the tune which became fainter with every passing second. She ended up standing amidst a forest. The place was remote and secluded with not even a single person in sight. The tune of the harmonica was also not there. Suddenly Ipsha saw there was something written on a faraway tree. She moved towards the tree and found a sentence written with chalk.

Are you ready for a little surprise?

Ipsha felt nervous as she read the word 'surprise'. She nodded her head and as she looked in another direction, she could see half a dozen photographs of her pasted on the trunk of a tree. She approached the tree and looked at the photographs where she looked very pretty. All the photographs were taken without her knowledge, but she looked extremely beautiful in the random pictures. Ipsha looked at each photograph with reverence. After looking at her own photographs, she wondered the photographer must be very talented.

Ipsha looked around, but couldn't see any hint of Arjun. She was, however, confident that he was nearby.

"Arjun! Arjun! Please come in front of me. I want to meet you." Ipsha shouted. The forest echoed her words. She repeated Arjun's name but all she got in return, were the echoes of her voice and the bland disappointment.

"Please don't disappoint me, Arjun. I am tired of waiting. Stop playing these games with me. If you are really fond of me, please come in front of me. I want to meet you. This wait is driving me crazy." Ipsha shouted again and again in desperation.

Finally, breaking the chains of her disappointment, Arjun appeared in front of her like a dream come true. Ipsha kept gazing at Arjun's striking face and physique as he approached her, with an alluring smirk on his face. She pinched her arm to believe that she was not dreaming with open eyes. She finally accepted with a nervous smile that the long wait has come to an end.

JUST ONE LOOK, THAT'S ALL IT TOOK

"Our eyes can deceive us because they are controlled by the mind. We often see what the mind instructs our eyes to see. "

"So, are you happy now?" Arjun said, breaking Ipsha's chain of thoughts.

Ipsha found her words gradually drying up in her tongue. Arjun's charismatic personality was more breathtaking than anything she has ever seen. None of her imaginations could come even closer to the reality of Arjun. She nodded her head with a smile as she gazed at him.

Arjun was extremely fair with hazel eyes that had the prowess to steal any heart he wanted. His chiseled jawline suited his flawless face. It was evident that he had recently shaved his face. Ipsha was sure that Arjun would look gorgeous even with stubble. She guessed him to be in his early or mid twenties.

Ipsha would have continued scrutinizing Arjun had Arjun not extended his hand towards her for a formal handshake. She extended her hand after taking a deep breath. Her cold palm felt comfortable in the warmth of Arjun's hand.

"Do I look scary, Ipsha? Why are you so quiet? According to my observation, you are a bold and talkative girl." Arjun said, moving a strand of hair from Ipsha's face with his other hand.

Ipsha still felt too tongue-tied to form a proper sentence. She shook her head and giggled timidly. Arjun ended up laughing as he saw the young girl nervous and excited at the same time. He pulled Ipsha closer to his chest and embraced her.

"I love your giggles." Arjun said, hugging Ipsha. He could feel her heartbeats racing when he hugged her.

"Now, say something, dear." Arjun said after letting Ipsha go from his arms.

Ipsha finally realized that being coy and reticent was not looking nice at all. She should break her quietude in order to look smart.

"Hi Arun! It's a pleasure meeting you." Ipsha mouthed.

Arjun sighed as Ipsha spoke the words, which made her laugh. She was astonished about how she could feel so comfortable with the person she was meeting for the first time.

In Arjun's handsome face, there was also a boyish charm which comforted Ipsha. Only his strikingly hazel eyes had an arcane aura in them. It seemed that Arjun could speak countless words with the intensity of his gaze. His eyes had it all in them: charm, mystery, allure and romance. Ipsha made up her mind to not look at those eyes as she felt she was getting hypnotized and carried away to a different world.

Arjun gestured Ipsha to sit on the grass. They sat on the green carpet and talked about each other's lives. Ipsha learned that Arjun is from Mumbai and his father is a businessman. They have many hotels across the length and breadth of the country under the name 'Walia group of hotels'. Arjun has recently joined his father's business and has come to Kalimpong for sightseeing.

The next hotel under the Walia banner would be set up in Kalimpong. So, he was staying in the remote hill station since the last two weeks. Ipsha further learnt that his father's rival, the Ahujas' are also eager to grab the land where they have planned to set up the hotel. There have been some constant legal problems associated with it. So, Arjun would be staying in Kalimpong for quite some time, unless the matter gets solved.

"I am sure that I am boring you with my family history. You tell me something." Arjun said, looking at Ipsha. As Ipsha shook her head, Arjun moved aside a strand of Ipsha's hair from her face. This seemed to be his new hobby, albeit an endearing one.

"I live with my sister, Akashi, who is seven years older to me. My parents passed away in a car accident four years back and since then, my sister is my guardian. I love her with all my life." Ipsha said, trying to hide her pain.

"You are a strong girl, Ipsha. I am sure Mom and Dad are always with you and your sister. Tell me one thing, you are a Christian, but on hearing your name, no one can guess that you are a Christian. How is that?" Arjun asked to divert Ipsha's mood.

"My mother was Bengali. She was from Kolkata, My mom and dad had an inter-religion marriage and so my mother's family had cut all ties with her after marriage. My mother gave us these sweet Bengali names: Akashi and Ipsha."

"This is beautiful. And I love your name." Arjun said, looking at Ipsha, making her blush.

"I thought you were a tourist here." Ipsha said.

"And what else did you think about me?" Arjun said, caressing Ipsha's right cheek. Ipsha lowered her gaze to conceal her coyness. Arjun probed her more to pull out words from her mouth. The nervous Ipsha finally spoke.

"I actually thought a lot about you, but you surpassed all my imaginations and thoughts." Ipsha said, looking into those hazel eyes that captivated her senses with every passing second. Arjun's lips broke into a smile as Ipsha uttered the words. She was delighted to see Arjun blush. It was unbelievable to see a powerful person like Arjun blush like a delicate flower. Ipsha held and caressed Arjun's hand to show her deep fondness.

Finally, Ipsha asked Arjun the question that she thought of asking him numerous times in her imagination. Earlier, she was hesitating as she was sheathed with an invisible layer of fear in front of Arjun. The conversations between them finally managed to vaporize that layer into nothingness. She asked him with impatience about when he saw her for the first time and how she caught his fancy.

"You did not catch my fancy, Ipsha. I fell in love with you. It's not a temporary infatuation or a chasing game. My feelings are as real as the beauty of Kalimpong." Arjun said, feeling hurt by Ipsha's choice of words. Ipsha was too young to fathom the reason for Arjun's pain. She smiled and waited for him to answer her questions.

Arjun grabbed Ipsha's hand and locked his fingers with hers. He smiled at the innocence of the young girl, who was extremely curious to know what made him fall in love with her.

"The day after I landed in Kalimpong, I did not have a lot of work. So, I went out for sightseeing. I was told by the local people that St. Augustine's school is one of the oldest and most famous schools in Kalimpong located amidst the hills. So, I decided to visit the good old school. It was during the break time when I visited your school and I am glad I did.

What caught my attention that day was a cute girl, who was imitating all her teachers and entertaining her friends by her amazing skill. I was amazed and couldn't take my eyes off that girl. I looked at her expressions and the joy she was getting when her friends applauded her for the mimicry. Right at that moment, one of her teachers pulled her ear from behind and she turned around totally speechless.

I couldn't control my laughter at that moment. All her friends ran away as soon as they spotted the teacher. The poor girl made an innocent puppy face and mouthed a feeble sorry to the teacher. I kept looking at the girl who turned from a bold entertainer to an innocent baby within the blinking of my eyes. Her teacher was still not convinced with her apology and so she touched her ears innocently. She kept on saying sorry, pouting her lips.

Finally, the heart of the teacher melted down and she forgave her. Right then, the girl was so overjoyed that she embraced her teacher tightly. She gave a flying kiss to her teacher and rushed into her classroom. That cute and innocent girl did not go alone into the classroom that day; she took my heart away with her. One look and that's all it took for me to fall in love with you." Arjun paused and winked at Ipsha.

Ipsha was stunned to hear the incident. She could never imagine that someone could find her silly antics charming and could actually fall for her, because of them. She looked at Arjun with surprised eyes as he continued speaking.

"From that day onward, I used to visit your school every day during lunch time so that I can see you. I thought you won't talk to me if I approach you directly. You would perhaps get scared and run away. So I used to follow you everywhere, enhancing your curiosity. On the third day, I learnt that your name is Ipsha when your friends summoned you.

I clicked many photographs of yours and gazed at them all the time. Every day, my attraction for you grew a bit more and I started following you to your home from school. I know the way I stalked you made you anxious and scared, but I also know that you started falling for me." Arjun paused and gazed at Ipsha's beautiful face, his gaze moving slowly from Ipsha's eyes to her lips. A strong desire emerged in his mind to kiss those beautiful rosy lips.

He caressed the lower lip of Ipsha and her slightly trembling lips further enhanced his desire to kiss them. As he studied her lips, her words jolted him out of his reverie.

"From whom did you get my number, Arjun? And today when I called that number, why did that person tell me that you are not available at that number?" Ipsha asked, unable to hide her curiosity. Now that Arjun has told her almost everything, she did not want any distance or secrets to exist between them.

"Rohan, your friend."

Ipsha gaped as Arjun mentioned Rohan's name. She couldn't believe that Rohan had given Arjun her number. Arjun laughed at her expression.

"Did anyone ever tell you that you are so expressive? Your expressions can evoke feelings, even in an inanimate object." As Arjun said the words, Ipsha laughed her heart out. The effervescent laughter of Ipsha made Arjun recall how he fell in love with this girl.

"I talked to Rohan one day on the road. I told him that I am a tourist and I lost my way. I needed to make an urgent call. He gave me his phone and I took your number from there, escaping his eyes. And I called you last night from the number of my hotel manager. So, my dearest, could I satiate your curiosity?" Arjun said.

Ipsha nodded as she was both happy and satisfied to know the answers to her questions. Whimsically, she stood up to Arjun's bewilderment. She ran to the tree where her photographs were stuck. She pulled out the photographs with childlike excitement and put them inside her bag.

"Can I please take these photographs? I never knew that I can look so good." Ipsha said looking at Arjun.

"Yes, my love." Arjun said nearing the trunk of the tree where Ipsha stood. The bright sunlight had ebbed down and the orange, evening sky looked prettier. The forest was isolated and Arjun couldn't stop himself from being close to Ipsha.

He placed his arms on the tree trunk in such a way that Ipsha was locked between his arms. She looked at Arjun in nervousness. His hazel eyes emanated love and longing, to which she wanted to surrender. Arjun inched closer to her, eradicating the distance between them.

Ipsha's timidity took over and she looked away from Arjun. Her breathing became heavier as she felt Arjun's breath on her neck. As she looked at Arjun, he sealed her lips with his without any delay. His hands moved from the trunk of the tree to her slender waist as he kissed her gently so that he doesn't scare her.

After a minute, he broke the kiss and looked into Ipsha's eyes. He could see a longing for him in those eyes instead of trepidation. He grabbed Ipsha by her waist and kissed her hard, this time. Ipsha gave into Arjun's whims and responded to the passionate kiss. She entwined her fingers around Arjun's neck as he moved his hands all over her. When the kiss ended, both of them looked at each other with a contented smile.

Arjun took Ipsha in his arms and ran his fingers through her hair. They stood there, totally lost in each other when all of a sudden, Ipsha shrieked.

"What happened?"

"My sister, Akashi must have reached home and she must be looking for me. It is already evening. I need to go home, Arjun right now." Ipsha said hysterically.

"Okay. Let's go and please calm down." Arjun said and walked with Ipsha towards her home.

ENCHANTED

"The world ceases to exist when you taste the feeling of love for the very first time. You are magically transported to a fairy-tale where angels sing the song of love and nothing matters except the two of you."

Arjun tried to hold Ipsha's hand as they were walking, but she shook her head, conveying her uneasiness. Arjun found it amusing and repeated it again and again, annoying Ipsha.

"Arjun!" Ipsha stopped walking and looked at Arjun, perplexed.

"Yes, Miss D'Souza." Arjun said with a smirk that lit his hazel eyes.

"If Akashi finds me holding your hand, she will kill me with her array of questions. In fact, you should leave now. My house is just a lane away and I do not want my elder sister to find me with you." Ipsha said looking at Arjun. Though Arjun's smile made Ipsha weak in her knees, she abstained from getting closer to him.

"Fine. I will leave. We will meet tonight after the town falls asleep." Arjun said and winked, which made Ipsha's jaw drop. Arjun looked at Ipsha's astounded face and chuckled. He pinched her flushed cheeks and waved her a goodbye. Ipsha stood still as Arjun walked away from her. The magical and erratic feeling took some time to settle under her skin. She felt happy and nervous at the same time. She wondered if she is crazily in love with Arjun. She finally could fathom why people associated the term craziness with love.

Ipsha ran towards her house, as she realized she has to face Akashi's questions. She could see Akashi standing outside the house with a flustered expression. Ipsha hatched a good excuse to present to Akashi and changed her excited demeanor into a casual one.

"Where have you been, all this while?" Akashi shouted as soon as she saw Ipsha.

"My paint tubes got empty. So, I went to the market." Ipsha said nonchalantly, but Akashi could smell something shady.

"It took you so long to get a paint box from the nearby market. You told Malati Masi that you would be back within an hour. Tell me what's wrong." Akashi said, nearing Ipsha.

On realizing that her elder sister was suspicious of her act, Ipsha tried to cover it up with deftness.

"Actually, I was getting bored at home. So, I was taking a stroll when I met a tourist couple. I talked to the wonderful couple and also clicked a few photographs of them. So, I think I got stuck there and lost track of time. I am so sorry, Akashi."

"Ipsha, you should not talk to strangers so cordially. I have told you many times." Akashi said with motherly concern. Ipsha was relieved that Akashi had believed in her lie. Her mission was accomplished. She was quiet as Akashi rebuked her because her mind was wandering in the direction of Arjun's thoughts.

Akashi was startled to see Ipsha smiling when she was admonishing her for her careless behavior. If it would have been some other day, then the rebel in Ipsha would have argued with Akashi. But today, Ipsha's wandering mind was too busy to concentrate on what Akashi was saying.

Akashi could clearly notice the change in Ipsha's behavior and thought to ask her about it. But she changed her mind as she thought it would exasperate Ipsha.

Akashi left Ipsha on her own after asking her how her day was at home. She could however, not ignore the restlessness that was growing in her heart. Akashi has been observing Ipsha's behavior for the last two days and she has found many changes that were hard to ignore. Akashi wanted to get to the root of it. She decided to talk to Ipsha's friends in the weekend.

A faint wish rustled in her heart to talk to Vihaan about Ipsha but she knew that she cannot tame such a yearning. Vihaan is a closed chapter. Talking to Vihaan would make her want him and leave her disheartened. She also thought that perhaps everything was alright and she was just over thinking. It can be that Ipsha is absolutely fine, but it's her care and love that is making her overly concerned.

Akashi sat in front of the synthesizer that Vihaan had gifted her on her birthday. Her broken heart and suppressed anger restrained her from playing it all these days. Tears raced down her cheeks as memories of Vihaan crawled back to her heart. Akashi played a few notes on the synthesizer with tear-laden eyes. As the melody of the notes reverberated in her ears, a huge burden in her heart seemed to ebb down. It was surprisingly liberating.

It is ludicrous why we human beings try so hard to conceal our tears. We fail to fathom that the more we camouflage our tears, the more we escalate the burden of grief in our heart. It is simple and wise to let the burden of grief metamorphose into tears and flow from our eyes. .

"It feels great to hear you play the synthesizer." Akashi couldn't realize when Ipsha came out of her room and stood beside her. She smiled at Ipsha.

"Are you fine? Does it hurt too much to play it?" Ipsha asked.

"To be honest, I thought it would break my heart into a million pieces, but I am surprised that I actually feel better after playing a few notes on it. That's the magic of music." Akashi said, wiping the few beads of tears on her cheeks. Ipsha took Akashi's hand in hers and squeezed it to assure her companionship.

"Fear often enslaves us, crumbling our sense of rationale and judgment. I was scared that playing the synthesizer will make me long for Vihaan and leave me heartbroken. But I am feeling so much better now. I think I have forgiven him. And now, I should try to move on." Akashi said the words with a ray of hope. Ipsha felt relieved to see the positive change in Akashi. She pleaded Akashi to sing a song. Akashi sang the song *"Someone like you"* by Adele and Ipsha could sense the agony in Akashi's beautiful voice.

Never mind, I'll find someone like you
I wish nothing but the best for you, too
Don't forget me, I beg, I remember you said
Sometimes it lasts in love, but sometimes it hurts instead

Akashi's eyes were clammy by the time she ended the song.

"Hey, my beautiful sister! You will find someone much better than Vihaan. Trust me." Ipsha said, wrapping her arms around Akashi.

Akashi smiled and thought whether her younger sister is capable of hiding something from her.

"Is there anything you want to tell me, Ipsha?" Akashi asked looking directly into Ipsha's eyes. Ipsha looked puzzled and started searching for words in the air. She felt as if her secrecy has been roughly unlocked. Her expression told Akashi that her doubts were not baseless.

"Nothing Lke that. Why did you ask?" Ipsha said after a few seconds.

"I thought I was too busy in my own world for a couple of days. I was desperately trying to get over Vihaan and so, I couldn't give you company." Akashi said calmly. Ipsha smiled and said that there was nothing that she was hiding from Akashi.

Ipsha was lying down on her bed that night when several thoughts pricked her one by one. She cursed herself for being a fool. She forgot to take Arjun's number and she also forgot to ask him the name of the hotel where he is staying. Basically, she knew nothing of Arjun and no possible way of meeting him or talking to him again. She was also afraid of how Akashi would react if she learned about the things that Ipsha had been hiding from her.

Ipsha remembered Arjun's departing words that they would meet that night, after the town falls asleep. Ipsha wondered if there was any truth in his words. She looked at the clock. It was 11 pm. Ipsha closed her eyes but her heart wandered with Arjun in the woods where they met. She could still feel Arjun's lips on hers. Her body coiled in shyness as she replayed the kiss again and again in her mind. Ipsha was barely asleep when her phone rang. She rubbed her eyes and answered the call in a sleepy voice.

"Come outside!"

"What?"

"Hey, this is Arjun. Come outside of your house for a while. I am waiting." Arjun's words were capable of driving away every bit of sleep from Ipsha's eyes. She got up from her bed hysterically.

"Are you serious?"

"Yes, sweetheart. I told you that we will meet after the town falls asleep. Did you think I was joking?" Arjun chuckled, much to Ipsha's surprise.

"You are a crazy man." Ipsha said with amusement.

"I am crazy for you. Now come outside. Make it fast."

"Give me a little time." Ipsha said and disconnected the call. She opened the window and saw Arjun's silhouette. She jumped in elation and rushed in front of the mirror. She wore a sweatshirt quickly on her top and untied her hair. She dabbed a little lip gloss to make sure she looked pretty. Before going outside, she tiptoed into Akashi's room. When she was convinced that Akashi was asleep, she got the confidence to step outside.

As Ipsha stepped outside, Arjun took her in his arms and lifted her up. Ipsha was transported to a different world as Arjun lifted her. She looked at Arjun's face, which was faintly visible in the moonlight. She kissed Arjun's forehead with palpitating heartbeats. Arjun smiled at Ipsha's gesture.

"I love you." Arjun said.

"I love you too, Arjun. Now put me down." Ipsha said and Arjun smiled. He held Ipsha tightly and kissed her lips. Ipsha felt surreal. Arjun's fragrance and the kiss made her forget the world around her. After about a minute, Arjun broke the kiss and landed her on the ground.

"Thank you." Arjun said.

"For what?"

"For coming outside. I wanted to give this to you. It's a small gift, or rather I should say a token of my love." Ipsha took the small paper bag that Arjun handed to her. She was immediately curious to know what was inside it.

"You are a gutsy girl." Arjun said, holding Ipsha's hand.

"If you are calling me gutsy, then what are you?" Ipsha said with a smile.

"My case is different. At midnight, a young high school girl is coming out of her house to meet her lover without fretting about her sister or neighbors. That is praiseworthy and it surely drives me crazy."

"My sister and neighbors are in their dreamland. So, I could take the risk. And which hotel do you stay that allows you to stroll around at midnight?" Ipsha asked.

"Everything is exceptional for Arjun Walia, my dear."

Ipsha rolled her eyes at Arjun's words.

Arjun smiled and told Ipsha that they would meet the next day. He insisted Ipsha enters her house before he leaves. He kissed her cheeks and waved her goodbye. Ipsha did as Arjun said.

After walking into her room, Ipsha realized that she has fallen crazily in love with Arjun. All she desired and wanted was Arjun. Arjun has become the synonym of happiness for her. She was totally enchanted by the man of her dreams.

RIPPLES IN THE STILL WATER

"When you throw a pebble into a still lake, you can see the ripples caused by it. Life is not like that still lake. The ripples of life cannot be seen, but can only be felt and the pebbles thrown at it cannot be understood, but can only be accepted with grace."

The creaking sound of the door when Ipsha came inside the house broke Akashi's slumber. Fearing that a thief has broken into their house, she rushed into the living room. In the dim light of the dining room, all she could faintly see was that the main door was locked. Akashi heaved a sigh of relief. She thought of checking if Ipsha is sleeping well. As she walked near Ipsha's room, she could clearly understand that Ipsha was awake. The light of her room was switched on.

Akashi peeped into Ipsha's room from the curtains and saw that Ipsha was unpacking a gift. At first, Akashi thought to ask Ipsha what was going on right away but then, she did not want to create a ruckus at midnight. She left Ipsha on her own and came back in her room. Although Akashi couldn't understand the exact thing, she could draw a faint sketch of the situation. Ipsha has been hiding quite a lot of things from her lately, which she needs to discover immediately.

Sleep eluded Akashi that night. Her peaceful heart was like the still water in a pond which was violently disturbed by Ipsha's behavior. The ripples formed in her heart were not allowing her to be at peace. She tossed and turned on her bed as scary thoughts enshrouded her mind. *Why is Ipsha not sharing things with me? Will this create a rift between me and Ipsha?*

The volley of questions made Akashi totally worn out. However, she knew what has to be done. With the lingering doubt and anxiety, Akashi finally fell asleep.

Ipsha couldn't help but ogle at the beautiful blue skater dress that Arjun had gifted her. After gazing at the pretty dress for a while, she decided to try it. Ipsha couldn't recognize her own reflection when she gazed at the mirror. The sleeveless blue dress accentuated her complexion and made her look very girly. Her wavy hair fell perfectly on her shoulders which made her look prettier than ever.

Ipsha fell in love with the girl she saw in the mirror. She fluttered her eyelashes and made cute faces in front of the mirror. *I think I have never looked so pretty in my life. I never knew I can also look pretty, like Akashi.*

Although Ipsha was not willing to change into her casual clothes, she hesitantly did so. She was excited with the fact that she would be wearing this dress and meeting Arjun the next day. As she was basking in her new found love and happiness, she remembered something. Akashi doesn't know anything about Arjun. She has to give some clever excuse to Akashi when she would be walking out in this beautiful dress the next day.

Aargh! Why can't I be happy without any problems? Why can't Akashi be happy for me? She is my sister after all.

As Ipsha soliloquized, she realized that she has not spoken a word about Arjun to Akashi. Therefore, blaming her sister won't be fair on her part.

But even if I would have told Akashi, she would have got enraged. She would have surely lectured me to stay away from strangers and to concentrate on studies. Tch!

Ipsha thought that she has done the right thing by keeping things under wrap. She would surely tell Akashi in such a way so that Akashi would understand that Arjun is not a stranger or a random guy. He is an established and independent person who loves Ipsha crazily. The thought was itself so saccharine that Ipsha couldn't resist smiling. She fell asleep with this beautiful thought.

When Ipsha woke up, she saw a message from Arjun. He told her to meet him at 12 pm for lunch at the Elgin Silver Oaks hotel. Ipsha blushed as she thought that this was their first official date. She gathered the confidence to lie to Akashi that she would be going out with her friends for lunch.

As she walked into the living room, she saw that Akashi was ready to go somewhere.

"Hey! Where are you going? You have off on Saturday." Ipsha asked.

"I have some urgent work, dear. I will be back by evening. You have your food on time and take care." Akashi gave a peck on Ipsha's cheek and rushed out of the house. Ipsha was glad that she won't have to convince Akashi with her lie. Now, she has all the liberty to dress up for her date with Arjun.

Ipsha painted her toenails and fingernails with a bright shade of royal blue as she listened to the songs of Enrique Iglesias on her iPod. Earlier, she used to dream of her hero when Enrique sang:

I can be your hero, baby
I can kiss away the pain
I will stand by you forever
You can take my breath away

Ipsha closed her eyes and thought about Arjun. Everything seems so surreal when it is Arjun. *I hope I am not dreaming the impossible or building hopeless castles in the air.*

She decided to tell Arjun to meet Akashi as soon as possible. That will give her come confidence about Arjun's intentions. At the same time, it would let Akashi know about the person with whom Ipsha is hanging around.

It was around 11.30 am when Ipsha was completely ready. She teamed the beautiful dress with a pearl pendant, pearl earrings and a pearl bracelet. It was a gift from Akashi on her sixteenth birthday. Ipsha applied some kohl and pink lipstick to look pretty.

She was content with her reflection in the mirror. She was sure that Arjun would be happy to see her in this dress. She thanked God that Akashi was not there in the house or else, her twinkling eyes and glowing face would have revealed the true story.

**

Akashi sat in front of Sandra in an authoritarian manner. Akashi was sure that Ipsha cannot keep secrets from her best friends, Sandra and Rohan. If something is cooking in Ipsha's life, they would be the first one to know about it and perhaps the only fools to encourage her about it.

"Sandra, if you are really Ipsha's true friend, then speak up." Akashi said the same thing for the third time now, her patience forsaking her.

"Sister, I am sorry, but Ipsha will never talk to me if I reveal any of her secrets." Sandra said with a silent sob, which annoyed Akashi further.

"Do you want Ipsha to be in some serious trouble? How will you feel if you know later that you could have saved Ipsha's life, but you didn't as you thought that she would stop talking to you?" Akashi asked holding Sandra's hand.

Sandra's mother insisted her to tell whatever she knows about Ipsha to Akashi. On her mother's insistence, Sandra decided to tell the truth. Sandra told Akashi about how a stalker was sending anonymous love notes to Ipsha, proclaiming his love for her. She also told that the stranger used to stroll around Ipsha's house in the wee hours of the night which scared Ipsha.

"My goodness! You are saying that a stranger used to stalk my sister around our house in the wee hours of the night. How could I not get any clue?" Akashi said with her palms on her forehead.

"I told Ipsha several times to tell about this dangerous stalker to you, but she did not listen." Sandra assured.

"And what else do you know about this creepy stranger? Please tell me all that you know. Does Rohan know anything else?" Akashi asked hysterically, unable to believe the news.

"Whatever I know, Rohan also knows that. Ipsha told us that the stalker used to play a tune on his mouth organ to assure Ipsha of his presence. Ipsha also said that she has seen his silhouette. He is a tall person who always wears a hat." Sandra said, recollecting every piece of information she could. Akashi felt giddy as she swallowed all of it. Akashi guessed that Ipsha was having an affair with someone from her school. But this was something she never imagined even in her dreams.

"Does Ipsha have any interest in that stranger or is she totally disinterested?" Akashi asked Sandra after gathering her composure.

"Actually, Ipsha was quite scared when she learnt that the stranger has followed her to her house. She used to stay disturbed and frightened. But.."

"But, what? Tell me." Akashi prodded Sandra.

"After Ipsha heard that tune, she got somewhat fascinated by the stranger. The disgust and anger that she earlier had for the stranger were strangely gone. I cannot say if she is interested in the stranger, but she desperately wanted to see him. This is something I am sure about." Sandra said confidently.

"I don't know where my sister got trapped into." Akashi's eyes were clammy as she thought about Ipsha.

"Thanks, Sandra. You have been a true friend of Ipsha." Akashi said and stormed out of Sandra's house.

When she reached home, she learned that Ipsha was outside. Her befuddled mind started thinking about every possible thing.

Is Ipsha with the stranger now? Is she safe? Are they dating each other? How should I deal with it? Please help me, God.

LOVE IS ALL AROUND

"Before a storm takes place, there are several signs: an uncanny calmness, a little flash, a hushed roar from the clouds. We realize something is wrong, but tend to ignore, not realizing how devastating the tempest can be."

When Ipsha reached the beautiful Elgin Silver Oaks Hotel, she was surprised to find the decoration of the table which was reserved for her and Arjun. She saw Arjun sitting on a chair and reading the newspaper, oblivious of her presence. Arjun looked charismatic in his white crisp shirt and navy blue jeans. Ipsha paused for a moment and pinched her left arm to ensure it was all real. As she opened her eyes after the silly act, she saw Arjun gazing at her, a little amused.

Ipsha felt embarrassed and bit her lower lip. Arjun approached her and gave her a beautiful bouquet of violet orchids and pink roses.

"You look stunning. You surpassed all my imaginations about how you would look in this dress. God! How can a person look as angelic as you?" Arjun said looking at Ipsha.

He took her right hand in his and planted a kiss there.

"Arjun, stop making me blush. I look average and just look at you, you look like some hero." Ipsha said, giggling.

"Beauty and modesty make an irresistible combination. By the way, do I look like a Hollywood hero or a Bollywood hero?" Arjun said, tilting his head a little.

"Well, let me think. You look more like a Hollywood hero with this amazing pair of eyes." Ipsha played along.

"Tom Cruise or Brad Pitt?"

"None of them. Somewhat like Robert Pattinson." Ipsha said with childlike excitement.

"So, you are a hardcore Twilight fan, ain't you?"

"Yeah. You can say so. I like Harry Potter, Twilight, Vampire Diaries and Chronicles of Narnia. Fantasy keeps me motivated and happy."

"That's a wonderful thing to know about you, angel. I will surely gift you all these movies and books." Arjun said as he ran his fingers through Ipsha's tresses. Ipsha smiled coyly, as she realized she had gotten gooseflesh on Arjun's touch.

Arjun directed her towards their table which was decorated with flowers and hearts. Ipsha was awestruck.

Arjun pulled the chair for her in a perfect chivalrous manner. Ipsha felt like a princess as she sat on the chair. Arjun's eyes did not leave her for a single minute.

"Stop gazing at me, Arjun. It's odd. Others are also looking at us." Ipsha said, feeling a little uneasy.

"Let them look." Arjun replied.

Ipsha smiled and looked away, thinking it's impossible to win with Arjun.

"You look so beautiful, Ipsha." Arjun said after heaving a long sigh of reverence.

"Come on! How many times will you tell me the same thing? You have seen better-looking girls in Mumbai or any other cities." Ipsha said.

"I swear I haven't come across anyone who is as beautiful

as you. And by the word beautiful, I mean beauty inside and out. Your charm, your innocence and your sweetness can put all the flowers in shame. Trust me I say every word from the core of my heart." Arjun said locking eyes with Ipsha.

For a fraction of a minute, I felt everything stood still there: the chill winds of the mountain, the chirping of birds and the people speaking around us. It was only Arjun and me, looking into each other's eyes as if we could see the entire universe in them.

Don't look at me in this manner, Arjun. It creates unusual symphonies in my heart and makes me forget myself. I no longer stay Ipsha, a simple mountain girl and sister of Akashi. I turn to something I am not. I turn to someone who knows nothing beyond you.

The spell was broken by the tune of the violin. Ipsha took her eyes off Arjun and looked around. She was delighted to find a musician playing a romantic tune in violin. Ipsha looked at Arjun who gave her a knowing smile. She rested her cheek in her palm and looked lovingly at Arjun.

"Did you like it?" Arjun asked.

"I loved it." Ipsha said.

"Can I have the pleasure to dance with you?" Arjun asked, extending his right hand towards Ipsha. Ipsha nodded after pondering for a few seconds. Arjun helped Ipsha to get up. He assisted her to keep her hand on his shoulder. Then, slowly but deliberately, he entwined his left hand around her slender waist. He could feel Ipsha's innocent trembling movements as he strengthened his grip. He pulled her closer towards him and they started dancing.

Ipsha was too shy to even look into Arjun's eyes. She matched his footsteps, lowering her gaze.

"Look at me. Look into my eyes, Ipsha." Arjun whispered.

Ipsha looked at Arjun in nervousness.

"This is perfect. Now we look like the world's best couple." Arjun said with a wink.

They danced for the next five minutes amid the scenic

beauty of the hills. The wind ruffled Ipsha's tresses and Arjun tucked them around her ear every time with sheer eagerness. The other people who were present in the hotel looked at the beautiful young couple with awe. The violin finally stopped, breaking the reverie of everyone.

Few people clapped after the beautiful performance. Ipsha felt overwhelmed by the attention. She sat on the chair and tried to register the things that happened.

I hope it's not a dream. Was I really dancing with Arjun so closely in front of all these people? Ipsha felt breathless as if she was running on a hilly road.

"Why were you so nervous, sweetheart?" Arjun asked after smiling at the people who clapped for their performance.

"This is my first couple dance ever." Ipsha said biting her lower lip.

"And you were outstanding. Your smell hypnotizes me. You smell so fresh and tranquil, like flowers." Arjun said. Ipsha's cheeks pinked.

Arjun ordered Chinese as Ipsha is extremely fond of Chinese cuisine. They had their food in silence.

Although Ipsha was silent, a thousand thoughts somersaulted in her mind. She argued with her mind if it would be right for her to bring those questions and thoughts in front of Arjun. On second thoughts, she did not want to lose the magical moments that she was spending with Arjun.

But what am I exactly to Arjun? Is he serious about me? Is he using me for a little entertainment during his trip?

"Are you alright? You look a little absent minded. Is the food not tasty enough?" Arjun asked as he caught Ipsha's faraway gaze.

Ipsha shook her head and looked into Arjun's eyes helplessly for him to read her thoughts.

"Have you done Paragliding?" Arjun asked excitedly, disregarding Ipsha's helpless look.

"Twice." Ipsha replied.

"Great! You are a brave girl. Promise me that you will accompany me to Delo, the place where the Kalimpong Paragliding Society is located. I want to try it soon." Arjun said to Ipsha with gleaming eyes.

Ipsha forced a smile on her lips as she was least interested in discussing paragliding. A thousand thoughts regarding their relationship were making her restless. Heaving a long sigh, she decided to ask Arjun some questions.

"What do I mean to you?"

Ipsha's blunt question discomforted Arjun.

"I love you, Ipsha. You know that already. Then, what kind of a question is this?"

"Yes, I know that. But, are you serious about me?" Ipsha asked.

"What are you trying to say?"

"Arjun, I am a simple girl who has never been to big cities. I live with my elder sister. I never had a boyfriend earlier. I thought love and romance happen in movies until I met you. You have taken over my heart and I am not under my control. It would break my heart into pieces if you forget me after you go back to your home. I hope I am not an object of entertainment in your trip." Ipsha said helplessly; insecurity and angst palpable on her face.

Arjun got up from his chair and sat beside Ipsha. He wrapped his arms around her and calmed her down, saying that he cannot forget her ever and that they will always be in regular touch. He promised to visit her in Kalimpong twice every year. Ipsha was somewhat appeased by Arjun's words.

"It would be great if you meet Akashi soon. She is my family and you know, she is the best sister anyone can ever have. She cares for me like a mother. I hate hiding things from her. Can you meet her someday at our house?"

"Will your sister be pleased to meet me? I don't think so." Arjun asked with a stern face.

"Of course! Why do you feel otherwise?"

"Just an intuition. It can spoil everything." Arjun said looking away.

"Akashi is a lovely girl. She can do anything for my happiness. Once she understands that you love me truly, she will approve our relationship." Ipsha said with optimism.

"Fine. Do what you wish. If your sister invites me, I will be your guest." Arjun said with a stoic face.

Ipsha was disappointed to see Arjun transform from warm to cold, within a few minutes. She thought that it was all her fault. She shouldn't have been so clingy and dependent.

"I am sorry." Ipsha mouthed.

Right then, a waiter accidentally tumbled a glass of water on Arjun's shirt as he cleaned the table.

"What the hell is this? Where is your manager? You people don't deserve to work in such a hotel." Arjun shouted his lungs out, which left Ipsha petrified. The waiter mouthed a feeble sorry. Ipsha could see the waiter shivering.

"You should go home now. I hope you liked the food." Arjun said, turning towards Ipsha.

Arjun's temper and sudden coldness made Ipsha numb. She couldn't say anything. Arjun accompanied her to the gate of the hotel and waved her a goodbye.

Please say something, Arjun. Don't leave me in this manner.

Ipsha's request remained unheard. Arjun retreated back to his room and Ipsha advanced towards her home. She did not expect it to end like this. The date which started on a bright note became murky in the end.

Helpless tears crawled down her eyes as she found herself locked in confusion. She wanted to sleep as she felt that a good sleep can eradicate all the negative thoughts from her mind. Ipsha was unaware that these were the faint signs of the turbulent storm that would be taking place in her life and change it forever.

THE RIFT

"When it is about the safety of her baby, a woman's intuition and gut feeling can never be wrong."

Ipsha tried to swallow her sadness as she reached her house. She knew that she cannot reveal the reason for her sadness to Akashi. Therefore, she put on a smiling mask with difficulty.

Ipsha greeted Akashi with a smile as she opened the door, but Akashi looked at her with a stern face.

"All okay?" Ipsha asked with a smile to which Akashi frowned.

"Where have you been all this while? You should inform me where you are going." Akashi's question was too direct for Ipsha. She felt awkward as she was not used to such authoritarian behavior.

"I was with my friends." Ipsha said casually and switched on the TV.

"Which friend?"

"Oh Akashi! What's wrong with you? It is weekend and I hang out with my friends every weekend. I was with Sandra and the gang." Ipsha answered with annoyance. Arjun's sudden cold behavior was already too distasteful for her to digest. Akashi's interrogation made her feel more miserable. Ipsha felt like escaping to the comfort of her room, but she was not lucky enough right then.

"I returned from Sandra's house just now. Stop lying and tell me the truth. Where were you? Who gave you this dress?" Akashi said, holding Ipsha by her shoulders. Ipsha was completely dumbstruck to find that her dishonesty has been caught red-handed by her sister.

She definitely wanted to tell Akashi the entire truth, but not in this manner, when she is forced and threatened. She wanted her own sweet time, but she knew that she was in troubled waters. The agony, anger and mistrust in Akashi's eyes pricked her heart.

Tears started rolling down her cheeks, but Akashi did not soften. She still had her eyes fixed on Ipsha, waiting for her to answer. Ipsha was startled to see that her tears did not soften Akashi even a bit. Akashi was determined to extract the truth from her.

"I was with Arjun. He gifted me this dress." Ipsha finally said helplessly after wiping her tears. She knew that this time, her sister won't wipe her tears with her fingers. Ipsha knew that she has caused pain to Akashi by hiding an integral truth from her.

"So, that stalker's name is Arjun." Akashi said in anger.

How did Akashi know about the stalking thing? Oh goodness! I guess Sandra had told everything to her.

Ipsha felt hollowness in her stomach as she realized how difficult it would be for her to explain Akashi. She wondered how to tell Akashi that she has fallen in love with Arjun, now that Akashi knows about the episodes of stalking.

"What were you doing with that stalker, Ipsha?" Akashi asked loudly, which terrified Ipsha.

"I love him, Akashi. Please try to understand. " Ipsha said with a helpless wail.

Akashi threw her arms in the air and looked at Ipsha with an unbelievable face as if she has said that she has seen a vampire in real.

"What do you understand of love? You are a school kid. You have your board exams next year. You better concentrate on studies and put this love stuff in the dustbin right now." Akashi shouted.

Ipsha couldn't believe Akashi's words. She couldn't fathom how her loving elder sister could disregard her feelings. Where on this earth, it is written that a seventeen-year -old girl cannot have true feelings for a guy? This statement of Akashi enraged Ipsha and broke her patience.

"I am not a kid, Akashi. I can have feelings for someone, the same way you have had feelings for Vihaan. You always knew that he was so wrong for you. You made a mistake by choosing a wrong guy. Therefore, you have no right to guide me in making my choices. Whether it is right or wrong, it's my life and my choice." Ipsha said hysterically.

Only after she has blurted out the words, she realized it was too insensitive of her to rub salt in Akashi's wounds. She looked at Akashi with an apologetic look, but it was too late. Words, once spilled cannot be taken back or altered at any cost. Words should always be measured and tasted before throwing on someone. Else it can cause a wound so profound that no words of consolation can make up for it ever.

When Ipsha looked at Akashi, she couldn't forgive herself. Akashi was wounded by the nail hitting words that Ipsha uttered. She was trying to suppress her sobs, but they were too loud to conceal.

"Since I made a wrong choice, I am trying to protect you from getting your heart tainted with scars." Akashi said amid her sobs.

I never wanted to hurt you, Akashi. I wanted to convince you about Arjun and me, but my tongue betrayed me. I am so sorry for bringing

*your break up with Vihaan in this context. Arjun is not like Vihaan.
I wish I could make you understand that somehow.*

Ipsha wanted to say these words aloud. Akashi's sobs were so unrelenting that Ipsha couldn't manage to speak a word. She walked into her room and buried her tear-stained face in the pillow which welcomed her heartily.

**

Ipsha didn't realize when she fell asleep. When she woke up, it was 2 am.

Oh God! I have been sleeping since the evening.

Ipsha rubbed her sleepy eyes and reached her cell phone. There were a couple of missed calls from Arjun and two messages. She read the messages without any delay.

The first message which was sent shortly after she slept, read:

I am sorry, Ipsha. I think I have been a little rude to you. Actually, I thought your sister won't approve our relationship. Therefore, I became insecure. I cannot afford to lose you, sweetheart.

The second message which was sent at midnight, read:

Please reply dear or pick up my phone. Don't be so upset and angry. I love you so much, trust me ☺

Ipsha smiled after reading the messages. She was glad that there was no distance between Arjun and her. She called Arjun at once and narrated him the entire sequence of events that took place after she reached home.

"You were right, Arjun. Akashi is completely against our relationship. I do not know how I will be able to convince her." Ipsha said sadly.

"I guessed it."

"The problem is that Akashi knows about the stalking part and now she presumes you to be a cheap stalker."

"Everything will be alright." Arjun reassured.

"Only after she will meet you. Let me see if I can convince her for that." Ipsha said.

"You have some food and go to sleep. It is quite late. I'll talk to you tomorrow. Goodnight." Arjun disconnected the phone without letting her speak. Ipsha wondered why Arjun always turn so cold whenever she talks about meeting Akashi.

Ipsha realized that she had a mild headache. She changed her clothes, had a little dinner that was kept on the dining table and went to bed.

Dear God, let tomorrow be a better day.

Ipsha slept, saying these words.

**

As Ipsha opened her eyes the next morning, she saw Akashi standing in front of her with a smile. Akashi has softened down from the shock of discovering her affair. Ipsha smiled at Akashi and Akashi pulled her in a motherly embrace.

The embrace was comforting for both Akashi and Ipsha.

"I am sorry. I was too harsh with you." Akashi said.

"I am sorry too, Akashi. I told you such insensitive words, which I regret every second. Please forgive me." Ipsha said genuinely. She had not expected her sister to mellow down the next day, as if someone has sprinkled some magic dust on Akashi when she was sleeping.

Akashi squeezed her sister's hand to assure her that everything is fine.

"I talked to Malati Masi and a friend of mine last night. Both of them told me that I treated you like a small kid. You are a grown up girl now. You will soon be eighteen. I must respect your choices and decisions. Being your guardian, I will obviously guide you, but imposing my choices on you is not right." Akashi paused and Ipsha looked at her eagerly, waiting for her to complete.

"The thing is that you are like my daughter, Ipsha. From the day mom and dad passed away, I have worn their shoes. I care for you not like a sister, but like my baby."

Ipsha's eyes were completely clammy by then. Overwhelmed with emotions, she snuggled with Akashi.

"I don't want you to get involved with someone who is dangerous and lethal for you. I cannot face my reflection in the mirror if I cannot protect you from any potential harm. I don't know how to explain you, but I am getting a bad intuition regarding this guy." Akashi paused and wiped her eyes. Heaving a long, tiring sigh, she concluded, "Perhaps, it's all a result of my over thinking."

"No Akashi. You trust me please, for once. Arjun is not lethal for me. He is an extremely caring, responsible and wonderful person. He cannot do me any harm. I agree that his technique of wooing me was a little odd, but he is not a cheap stalker. He is really nice." Ipsha said with a convincing tone. Akashi could comprehend how much her younger sister was smitten with this guy.

"I want to trust you, dear. Out of all things, the last thing that I would want is that an irrevocable and dangerous rift forms between us. You remember what we promise to each other on our birthdays. No matter what happens, we will always support and be with each other." Akashi said looking at Ipsha who nodded her head.

"I would like to meet Arjun. Invite him to our house for dinner today. Today is Sunday and I have all the time to prepare a meal for him." Akashi said with a smile. Ipsha loved the idea. That's what she wanted all the while. She was confident that once Akashi meets Arjun, she will be freed from all the negative thoughts about Arjun.

Ipsha hugged Akashi and told her that she is the world's best sister

"I will call Arjun right away. And I will assist you in preparing the meal. Thanks a ton." Ipsha said to which Akashi smiled.

"Finally, I could cheer you up." Akashi said and went to the kitchen

Ipsha stood still and thought how she could say such venom stained words to Akashi the other day. This woman has devoted her life towards Ipsha's well-being. Akashi has always treated Ipsha like her baby. Ipsha remembered how Akashi would stay awake the entire night whenever she had fever. Akashi would keep checking her temperature the entire night, abandoning her sleep and food.

How insensitive of me to accuse my sister of her choices and hurt her intentionally! Akashi has forgiven me because she is such a wonderful person. I am sure if Mom and Dad were alive today, they would have never forgiven me for my selfishness.

Ipsha was happy that the rift between her Akashi was mended by their love for each other.

Ipsha dialed Arjun's number and greeted him with a chirpy voice.

"It is such a pleasure to hear your happy voice, Ipsha." Arjun said with a smile.

"Yes! I am so happy. Guess what?"

"What?"

"Akashi wants to meet you. Today. For dinner. Isn't it great? You are cordially invited to our house." Ipsha giggled.

"Okay." Arjun responded. Ipsha was slightly disappointed by the meek answer.

"Ipsha, what's the hurry to meet your sister so soon?"Arjun asked.

"What is your problem to meet her? She is my only family and the person I am closest to. Understand. " Ipsha tried to explain Arjun in broken sentences. She wanted to say so much, but she stopped.

"Hey, don't get me wrong. We started dating each other on Friday and on Sunday, you want me to meet your sister. There is nothing to rush. I worry things between us can spoil. But, if that makes you happy, I will be glad to meet her." Arjun said, calming Ipsha.

"See you then." Ipsha said softly. Few questions were

disturbing her.

Why Arjun always gets upset whenever I tell him to meet Akashi? Why doesn't he try to understand how close I am to Akashi? Is he not serious about me?

"See you, princess." Arjun said cheerfully.

"I hope you know my address. Do you require directions?' Ipsha asked in an absent-minded way.

"You forgot that I used to stalk you around your house." Arjun chuckled as he completed his words. It made Ipsha laugh too. Finally, the ambiance got lightened.

Both Ipsha and Akashi looked forward to Arjun's visit.

BITTERSWEET

"Love is a misunderstood term. Love flowers with the passage of time. What often happens is a fervent attraction, followed by a passionate attachment. Most of the times, we read this attachment as love and cling to it."

Ipsha greeted Arjun outside her house at 6 pm. She wore a fitting, white woolen top and a pair of blue denims. She left her hair open and teamed her outfit with white loops. Ipsha convinced Akashi that she would greet Arjun at the lane as he has never been to their house.

Ipsha forgot that Akashi knew everything about Arjun's stalking. She did not even wait for Akashi's affirmation; she read her silence as yes. Akashi was keen to meet the guy who has changed her sister drastically within a few days. She mentally prepared herself to exhibit a good amount of patience with both Ipsha and Arjun.

When Ipsha cast her eyes on Arjun, she was bewitched once again. Arjun looked jaw-dropping in the lavender shirt, blue blazer and black trousers. Ipsha had no idea that he could look so breathtakingly handsome in formals. As she neared him with a saccharine smile, she could smell his cologne that tempted her to bury her nose in his chest. Gathering herself, she said a soft hello.

"I thought I was nervous. But here, Miss Ipsha is so timid and quiet. What's wrong with you? Your sister must have scolded you for greeting me here, right?"

Ipsha shook her head and looked around to see if anyone is visible. On being sure that no one is watching them, she hurriedly kissed Arjun on his lips.

"I love your unpredictability!" Arjun said with a smirk, after recovering from the sudden kiss.

Ipsha blushed and told him that there is no need to worry about Akashi. She told him to be cool and casual with Akashi. She also told him not to display any affection in front of Akashi.

"I will remember. Now, shall we proceed?" Arjun asked Ipsha, dreading that she would soon give him a list of do's and do not's when meeting Akashi.

Arjun followed Ipsha to her house. They did not exchange any words in the 2 minutes' walk. Both of them were busy in their own thoughts. The front door was kept open for their convenience. Ipsha took Arjun to the living room and told him to take a seat. Akashi was nowhere visible. Malati Masi brought a tray of coffee and cookies within the next five minutes.

Ipsha was happy with the hospitality that was provided to Arjun.

"Hey, you enjoy the coffee. I will be back within a minute." Ipsha said to Arjun and he nodded.

Ipsha saw Akashi busy in making the dinner arrangements in the kitchen. On noticing Ipsha, Akashi smiled. Ipsha saw that Akashi had worn a lemon yellow short *kurti* and jeans. Her hair was neatly tied in a ponytail and her earrings dangled cheerfully. She looked effervescent.

"Won't you meet him? I thought you are eager to meet

him." Ipsha asked excitedly.

"Yes, I am. Let's go." Akashi smiled at her sister's excitement and walked towards the living room.

Akashi spotted Arjun from a distance. His outfit gave her the impression that he is suave, rich and polished. Akashi greeted him with a smile.

"I think I have seen you somewhere. Your face looks familiar." Akashi said after looking at Arjun's face for a minute.

Arjun laughed at the remark and shrugged his shoulders. Ipsha found Akashi's remark a little weird and disregarded it at once. The three of them indulged in conversation, but Akashi's mind was hugely disturbed. Arjun's countenance made her restless. She racked her mind again and again, but couldn't place him.

"Say something, Akashi. I thought you are going to interview Arjun today but it's only Arjun and I talking throughout the evening. Why are you so absent-minded and quiet?" Ipsha asked.

"I think your sister is not well. She should rest. Arjun suggested.

"Guys, I am absolutely fine. Arjun's face is so familiar that my mind was wavering." Akashi explained.

"You know I had once read somewhere that we all resemble at least 7 people on this earth. Just imagine! I am sure you have come across one of the 7 doppelgangers of Arjun." Ipsha said and laughed at her own joke. Akashi and Arjun were quiet.

"Arjun, my sister is a wonderful singer. She plays the synthesizer too. You must hear her someday. Akashi, you will be glad to know that Arjun is also very inclined towards music." Ipsha tried to find some common connection between her sister and love interest to break the ice.

"I would love to hear you, Ma'am." Arjun said looking at Akashi.

"We are almost of the same age. So please call me by my name. Don't make me feel so old." Akashi said with a smile. Arjun and Ipsha laughed and the ambiance lightened.

"We should have dinner first and then we can have a short musical session." Akashi said to which both Ipsha and Arjun agreed.

The three of them settled for dinner. Akashi had prepared chili chicken and mixed noodles for Arjun. Ipsha told her that Arjun is fond of Chinese cuisine. Akashi has always been a great host. Ipsha was sure that her sister would prepare a wonderful dinner. Ipsha signaled Akashi that the dinner was extremely delicious. Arjun was too busy with the food to notice the silent conversation between the sisters.

"The meal is sumptuous." Arjun said after a few minutes. Akashi smiled and Ipsha kept speaking of Akashi's culinary skills. She always got happiness by bragging about her sister's talent, be it cooking or singing. Arjun patiently listened as he finished his food.

"How many days are you staying in Kalimpong, Arjun?" Akashi asked.

"At least two more weeks. Can be longer too. Even if I go back, I will come back here again within a few weeks because of business purpose." Arjun said.

"Ipsha told me about the hotel that your company would be building here. Where is the site?" Akashi prodded further.

"At the last turn of Rinkingpong Road. The place is quite deserted right now." Arjun replied confidently. Akashi tried to gauge his words. She nodded with a smile to every answer that Arjun gave. Her mind was stuck on other things such as the strange familiarity of Arjun's face. She also had an intuition that something is badly wrong.

"What is your father's name, Arjun?" Akashi asked again.

"Akhilesh Walia." Arjun said, a little annoyed with the volley of questions thrown at him.

"Akashi, now stop your questions. Let us enjoy the

dinner." Ipsha came to Arjun's rescue. She could sense Arjun's annoyance. Akashi nodded and kept quiet. Ipsha started blabbering about a variety of things. Arjun and Akashi replied in monosyllables when they had to.

After the silent dinner, Ipsha guided Arjun to the wash basin located in the corridor between the living room and the kitchen.

"Ipsha, I should go back to my hotel now. Your sister seems a little offended by me." Arjun said as he washed his hand.

"No, Arjun. It's not like that. Akashi is not so outspoken like me. She measures her words before saying. She is not much of a talker. She likes you, I am sure. See, how wonderfully she has prepared the dinner for you." Ipsha said.

Arjun shrugged his shoulders with a meek smile. On reaching the living room, Ipsha and Arjun saw Akashi in front of the synthesizer. She was getting ready for the music session that she promised before the dinner. Ipsha was happy that Akashi wanted to spend more time with Arjun.

"Hey Arjun, join me." Akashi said, looking at Arjun.

Arjun nodded with a smile. Akashi started playing a beautiful tune on her synthesizer. Arjun was impressed by her command over the synthesizer. Akashi started singing, mesmerizing Arjun and Ipsha with her mellifluous voice.

I gaze deep
Into your charcoal eyes
Watch my reflection
In silence, in wonder!

Arjun sang along. Ipsha watched Akashi and Arjun with reverence as they sang together.

In that intense eye lock
Our souls seem to blend
If eyes could speak
Ours would have sung instead of said.
Tell me it's not a dream

Tell me it's not a fairy tale
How to confide, I haven't got a clue
Oh yes, but I want to trust you!

Ipsha clapped after the song ended.

"You both are so talented." Ipsha said.

"Your sister is really talented, Ipsha. She has a gifted voice. The way she sang with the synthesizer was praiseworthy, especially the way she started the song…oh my God!" Arjun said looking at Akashi with reverence.

"Even you sang beautifully with me." Akashi said to Arjun.

Ipsha was delighted to find Arjun and Akashi admiring each other

"You both are so talented. You sound like a successful team. Give it a thought to make music together, someday." Ipsha said.

"Stop it, Ipsha. We are no professionals." Akashi said, disregarding the idea at once.

Ipsha was relieved that the two favorite people of her life could finally get along with each other.

"Akashi, can I show Arjun the paintings in my room?" Ipsha asked.

"I think we should leave Arjun now. It's 10pm and he needs to return to the hotel."

"Just two minutes." Ipsha pleaded and pulled Arjun to her room.

As they were in the privacy of each other, Ipsha held Arjun firmly and kissed him.

"Sweetheart, I knew it well that you pulled me to your room to kiss me and not for showing your paintings," Arjun said breaking the kiss.

Ipsha frowned at his remark.

"Sorry. Come here. See my paintings. Aren't they nice?" Ipsha said, pulling Arjun to the corner of her room where her paintings rested on the wall.

"They are out of the world. You create magic on your canvas." Arjun said, looking at the paintings.

Ipsha smiled at the compliment. She could soon sense Arjun's lips on her nape teasing her. As she turned, Arjun devoured her lips with all his love and longing for her. They separated in an instance as they heard the sound of footsteps.

"Yes, Arjun you should go now. Goodnight." Ipsha said loudly as she heard the footsteps. Akashi entered the room and agreed with Ipsha. The two sisters waved goodbye to Arjun after he thanked Akashi for the wonderful dinner.

Akashi was happy, but the doubt regarding Arjun did not leave her mind. It was a bittersweet meeting.

Knots Left Behind

"Illusion and deception are two confusing terms, which are too hard to distinguish at times. In the former, we are responsible for seeing a mirage and in the latter, we are forced to see a mirage.

Arjun rushed to the lobby of the hotel with a bewildered look on his face. He was startled to know that Akashi D'Souza has been waiting for him since the last one hour. Arjun wondered why Akashi came to meet him at the crack of dawn.

Dreading if Ipsha is alright, Arjun did not even care to wash his face. He reached the lobby after putting on a shirt. The lobby was empty except for the receptionist who was working on some documents.

"Good morning." Arjun said nearing Akashi, who looked different from the last day. She looked sleep deprived and the color in her face has totally run off. She wore the same yellow *kurti* that she wore the last day, but her hair was not tied. It was unkempt that made her look haggard. There were dark circles under her eyes which revealed that she did not sleep well last night. Arjun wondered what could have made her so befuddled.

"What is your real name?" Akashi asked without caring to exchange any pleasantries with Arjun.

"Sorry! I didn't get you." Arjun said, shocked by the question.

"You are not Arjun Walia. Akhilesh Walia, the famous businessman has a son, Arjun Walia but he is only sixteen years old. He is currently doing his schooling in New York. That's what the internet told me last night when I conducted a research on you." Akashi paused. Her eyes were stern which demanded an honest answer.

Arjun looked sideways and shook his head. He couldn't believe that this lady has disrobed the veil of deception so swiftly from his face.

"I cannot believe that you researched about me all night. That was quite quick." Arjun said, rubbing his jaw.

"I wouldn't have if your face did not bear that strange familiarity. After brain storming the entire night, I could finally recognize that face. And after I recognized, peace eluded me." Akashi said angrily.

"What are you exactly? A goon, a thief or a robber? Six months back, in the Howrah Railway station, a bunch of goons was running away after some crime. When the police was about to catch one of them, the man took hold of a girl in the railway station and pointed his knife at her. He dragged her with him till he entered the train. Then, escaping the eyes of the policemen, he threw her in the station from the train. Yes, I was that girl who was traumatized in that incident and the rowdy goon I am talking about is you." Akashi said looking straight into Arjun's eyes.

Arjun stood silent.

"It was really hard to recognize you. At the railway station, you looked exactly what you are: a goon or a thief. But yesterday in your formal wear and polished look, you looked like a businessman. What are you up to? Why have you chosen Ipsha as your victim? Why are you here, out of all places? What do you exactly want?" Akashi asked the questions, one after the other.

Arjun closed his eyes as Akashi kept questioning him.

"I want an answer, right now." Akashi said, a little louder. The receptionist looked at Akashi sensing something is wrong. Akashi smiled at her and signaled that everything is alright.

"Please give me an answer." Akashi persisted.

"Yes, you are right. I am not Arjun Walia from Mumbai. I am no way related to the Walia Group of Hotels. I cannot reveal my identity to you for obvious reasons. But the one thing I can assure you at this moment is that I truly love Ipsha. She is not a victim." Arjun paused and looked at Akashi, who looked as angry as she was before he started speaking.

"I have come to Kalimpong for two purposes. One for my work and second for finding out if you know anything that can be harmful to my team. When we bumped into each other at the station, I accidentally dropped an important thing. I doubted that I left it in your bag. This was the reason I started stalking you around your house. I kept an eye on your every move, but after some days, I was convinced that you don't know anything. In the process, I fell in love with your sister. This is no deception." Arjun said, leaving Akashi speechless.

"What? You were stalking me? And, what did you think you left in my bag?" Akashi fumbled. All these revelations were too much for her to grasp.

"You don't need to know that, Akashi. Just know that I love Ipsha. Your sister is in safe company. I will die rather than harm her ever. Somehow, I knew that you would identify me and object to this love affair. Therefore, I tried to avoid meeting you. But, I gave away my inhibitions for

Ipsha's happiness."

"What else do you expect me to do? Allow my sister to date a criminal who has once left me traumatized. I beg you to leave Ipsha and go away from our lives. Or else, I will tell Ipsha everything and also report you to the police of Kalimpong."

The last words of Akashi enraged Arjun. Here, he is politely explaining to this woman how much he loves Ipsha and despite understanding, she is warning to drag him to the police.

"Miss, D'Souza, don't read my gentleness as helplessness. I love Ipsha and I am being nice to you for her sake. You can do anything you want. Your warnings or threats won't cripple my love for Ipsha." Arjun said with a grimace.

"Ipsha won't like to see your face once she knows your identity." Akashi challenged.

"Do whatever you want." Arjun said and walked towards his room.

Akashi stood like a stone for a few seconds, unable to decipher what she should do. Suddenly, she ran towards Arjun and blocked his path by standing in front of him.

"I don't have anyone in this world except Ipsha. Therefore, if you cause my sister any harm, be sure that I won't leave you." Akashi said hysterically holding Arjun's collar.

Arjun removed Akashi's hands off him and walked inside his room. He knew that he loved Ipsha and there was no stain on his love. He would have talked to Akashi nicely only if she would have given him an opportunity instead of a warning.

Without any delay, he dialed Ipsha's number.

**

Akashi felt helpless as she saw Arjun walking away.
Can Arjun or whatever his name is, lure Ipsha with his lies?
Won't Ipsha trust me, her own sister?

92

What could have Arjun left in my bag that day?

Akashi made a mental note to check her bags and belongings for a clue that could help her take a stand against Arjun. The passion that Akashi has read in Ipsha's eyes conveyed that it won't be easy for her to convince Ipsha to stay away from Arjun.

Will Ipsha believe me if I tell her about Arjun's reality?

Akashi felt sick and feverish with her thoughts.

"Are you alright?" The kind receptionist asked on noticing Akashi's unsteady gait.

"Water." Akashi managed to reply. Her throat has dried up and she realized she needed some water.

The receptionist offered Akashi a bottle which she took greedily. After finishing half of it, she felt better. She knew that she had to tell Ipsha everything that she knew. Ipsha would be shocked, but she will surely confide in her.

Akashi started walking towards her house as she prepared what she would exactly tell Ipsha. Her feet felt heavy as she was overburdened with thoughts. People on the street looked at Akashi as she walked like an aimless person, her steps unsteady.

At that moment, Akashi felt a strong urge to call Vihaan. She needed to confide. She needed someone who knows her and Ipsha, someone who won't be judgmental and yet listen to her. She missed Vihaan terribly. More than a boyfriend, she missed the ever supporting friend in Vihaan. She knows that Vihaan is irresponsible, but she cannot deny that Vihaan is a wonderful friend.

It is said that when two people are connected by heart, they have a telepathic connection. The heart emits some invisible waves whenever one person starts missing the other. The other person, on getting the wave understands that he or she is being missed. This is the best explanation that Akashi could give herself when she saw her phone ringing at that moment.

"Hello!" Akashi said softly after answering the phone.

"Hey, Akashi!" Akashi recognized the voice at once. She could not believe that Vihaan called her right at the moment when she was missing him terribly.

"Long time! It feels so good to hear your voice. How are you, my girl?" Vihaan said in his usual upbeat voice.

The word *my girl* made Akashi emotional. She started sobbing.

"What's wrong, Akashi? Is Ipsha alright?" Vihaan asked as he heard her sobs.

"I don't know, Vihaan. I feel I have lost my sister. I have not been a good elder sister and guardian of Ipsha. I feel so lonely and weak today." Akashi said amidst her sobs.

"Please tell me what the matter is." Vihaan insisted.

"Nothing serious. We had a small quarrel." Akashi said, gathering her composure. She decided not to tell Vihaan the truth, now that they have parted ways. She did not want to sound needy.

"Everything will be fine. You know how Ipsha is. She would get angry and hyper for a few minutes and then she would cuddle you and say sorry." Vihaan consoled Akashi.

"Right." Akashi agreed.

"And hey, you are the most amazing and loving person one can have as a sister and a friend. Your sacrifice, love and care have no limits. Never forget these words, Akashi. You have a heart of gold." Vihaan's words were like a soothing balm on Akashi's weary mind.

"Thank you, Vihaan. Thanks for calling. It means a lot." Akashi said with a smile.

"I am always there for you, Akashi. Please don't hesitate to call me ever. Take care."

"You too."

After talking to Vihaan, Akashi felt much better. She saved Vihaan's number again and felt glad that he cares for her. A few soothing words from someone we love at the time of despair can produce a magical, healing effect on us.

Once again, Akashi realized how much she loves Vihaan despite not being in a relationship with him. Sometimes, when the love is profound, a relationship is nothing more than a name tag. The thing that matters is how the person we love makes us feel. The feeling is so precious and beautiful that it overshadows every other thing.

TRUTH IN YOUR EYES

"Decisions taken in haste are seldom right, the same way promises made in euphoria are hardly kept."

Arjun and Ipsha stood in front of the Watershed View Point. This place had a great view of the most scenic golf course in the country. However, Ipsha and Arjun were too worried to bask in the scenic beauty of Kalimpong.

Ipsha was unaware why Arjun looked so devastated. She was startled when Arjun called her early in the morning, his voice low and melancholic.

"Can you please meet me at the Watershed View Point within thirty minutes? It's urgent." Arjun had asked.

"What's wrong, Arjun?" Ipsha was surprised.

"I love you, Ipsha. Please don't ask me any questions. Please meet me right now." Arjun pleaded.

Sensing that something is terribly wrong, Ipsha put on a jacket over her top and ran towards the Watershed View Point. She did not even care to comb her hair. On her way, she used her fingers to untangle her tresses. It was easier for Ipsha to get out of the house as Akashi was not there. She told Malati Masi to tell Akashi that she had gone to meet Arjun as it was urgent.

Ipsha waited for Arjun to speak, but he was quiet. Both of them looked towards the golf course, but none of them said a word.

"Arjun!" Unable to exhibit any more patience, Ipsha held Arjun's arm. When he turned towards her, she was surprised to see his eyes red and clammy. He looked lost and anguished.

Ipsha wanted to embrace him tightly, but she resisted as there were a few people around them.

"What has happened? Why do you look so pathetic?" Ipsha said, holding Arjun by his shoulders.

"I am sorry, Ipsha. I am not the right guy for you. I should go away from your life." Arjun said and looked away from her.

"Did Akashi tell you anything? You both got along well yesterday, then why do you speak such horrible words? Don't you realize how badly your words are hurting me?" Ipsha said, panicking.

"Akashi knows the truth. You don't know it."

"Which truth are you talking about?"

"About my identity."

"Your identity? You are Arjun Walia. Right?" Ipsha asked in confusion.

"I lied to you, Ipsha. If you would have known my real identity, then you would have never fallen in love with me. So, I deliberately lied to you. But I realize that I have built castles in the air all through this time, which will break one day. Once you know the truth, you will not care about anything and despise me. I shudder to think how I can tolerate that loathsome look in your eyes for me. It will break my heart into a million pieces. I should listen to your sister and just go away from your life." Arjun said.

All these revelations were too much for Ipsha to digest at

a time. She was confused and tried hard to comprehend Arjun's words.

"Please don't scare me, Arjun. I beg you." Ipsha said, jitters running down her spine.

Arjun neared Ipsha and cupped her face with his hands. He looked into her eyes directly and said, "I have never been as scared in my life as I am right now." A tear drop trickled down his eyes, cementing the truth in his words.

"Don't be. I love you. I will always be by your side, no matter who you are. The only thing that matters to me is your love." Ipsha said in a nervous voice. Arjun was relieved by the assurance that Ipsha provided him.

"My name is Arjun Sharma. I was born to poor parents in a small district near Kolkata called Konnagar. My father worked as a security guard in an English medium school. One fateful day, he lost his limbs in a fatal accident when he was returning home.

After my father's accident, my mother was compelled to work in other people's house as their domestic help. Since a very young age, I realized that the world runs on money and nothing else. I saw my little newborn sister succumbing to the pains of hunger and dying eventually.

I was a bright student, but the poverty of my family used to keep me restless all day and night. I used to constantly think of ideas of making money. It was during my high school days that I came across Mr. Basu. I was almost run over by his car and so he decided to drop me to the hospital. As fate permitted, he developed a sort of liking towards me. On knowing about my poor financial condition, he offered me a lucrative job, but it was illegal.

I learned that Mr. Basu is one of the most powerful people of Kolkata. He is the richest man in the city and is involved in many illegal activities such as drug trafficking. I wanted money desperately and he wanted a loyal servant. I started working under him from that day. Although the work was illegal, it paid me royally. All my financial problems dissolved and I became his loyal servant.

I have come to Kalimpong for his work. I camouflaged my identity not only to you, but also to the place where I am staying. When Mr. Basu learned that Walia group of industries are setting a hotel here, he told me to go with the identity of Arjun Walia so that the police cannot suspect anything. The name that I have entered in the hotel registration is also Arjun Walia whereas, in reality, I am Arjun Sharma." Arjun paused and looked at Ipsha who stared at him with a helpless face.

"Your sister had seen me once in Howrah Railway Station. I bumped into her when I was running away from the police. I wonder how she could recognize my face. Her doubts got cleared when she researched online about Walia Group of Industries and found out that I am not Arjun Walia." Arjun said with honesty. He was aware that the only one thing that can keep Ipsha with him is being truthful.

Ipsha fidgeted with her jacket. She found herself lost in the zone where lies and truth got overlapped.

"Say something Ipsha for God's sake." Arjun said, holding Ipsha.

"I don't know what to say," Ipsha said as tears crawled down her cheeks.

Arjun looked at Ipsha, hurt. He felt betrayed by her answer.

"Fine. You can go to your home. This was the last time we met." Arjun said stoically.

Ipsha stood like a statue and watched Arjun walk away from her. A volley of questions pricked her all at a time. She closed her eyes in search of some respite.

Should I trust this guy, who had lied to me?

How can I love a person who is involved in illegal activities such as drug trafficking? How can I love a person who is being chased by the police, every now and then?

Should I go back home, to Akashi's arms and forget this guy forever?

What about the love that I have seen in his eyes, intense and profound for me?

Isn't it more important that Arjun loves me truly than the fact that he is into illegal activities, due to his family's financial conditions?

Should I let Arjun go away from me?

Can I live without Arjun?

When she opened her eyes, she knew what she wanted, but Arjun was nowhere in sight. She looked for him all around the place, but he was gone.

With tears streaming down her eyes, she ran towards the Elgin Silver Oaks Hotel.

When she reached his hotel, she asked the receptionist about Arjun's room number.

"Ma'am, we cannot give our guest's room number without his permission. Can you please wait for a while? We will call him to confirm." The receptionist said as politely as possible. Ipsha had no other options apart from nodding and praying to God that Arjun meets her.

After calling Arjun, the receptionist gave his room number to Ipsha. She thanked her with a smile amidst her palpitating heartbeats and rushed towards Arjun's room. Arjun opened the door before she knocked it.

Arjun and Ipsha gazed at each other in silence until Ipsha threw her arms around Arjun's shoulders. Tears crawled down her cheeks, which showed no signs of stopping. Arjun was startled but relieved at the same time. Taking Ipsha in his arms, he locked the door.

"Why are you crying?" Arjun whispered in Ipsha's ear, without breaking the hug.

"I love you, Arjun. I cannot lose you. I don't have many people in my life. After Akashi, it's you who loved me so much and painted a rainbow in my life. If you walk away, my life will be like a barren desert. I am not good at handling separation. I already miss my parents so much. I cannot bear the pain of separation from you."

"I am not good for you, Ipsha." Arjun said, wiping Ipsha's tears with his index finger.

"It doesn't matter to me if you are the son of a businessman or someone involved in drug trafficking. I love you." Ipsha said.

Arjun took Ipsha in his arms as a plethora of emotions washed over him. He was happy that it was not only he who was afraid of losing Ipsha. Ipsha also feared the same.

Arjun kissed Ipsha like there is no tomorrow. He claimed her lips and she gave in to his silent demand. He took off her jacket and kissed her on her nape.

"Please don't go away from me ever. You are mine." He whispered on her ears.

Before Ipsha could say a word, he lifted her gently and perched her on the bed. As he showered endless kisses on her neck and shoulders, Ipsha murmured sighs of pleasure. She pulled him closer to her and kissed him passionately. Arjun's lips on hers, his skin against hers and his hand running all over her body felt surreal. She rolled over Arjun and climbed on top of him.

Ipsha unbuttoned Arjun's shirt and kissed him with fervent passion. She was lost in him and didn't realize when she slept eventually in his arms.

When she woke up, she saw Arjun gazing at her.

"Goodness! I slept. Why didn't you wake me up?"

"I loved watching you sleep so innocently, snuggled to my chest. This is the sweetest thing that I have ever seen." Arjun said with a smile.

How are you so charming, Arjun? Whenever I look at you, I can feel my heart skipping a beat.

Ipsha thought, looking into Arjun's eyes. She smiled at her thoughts and gave a peck on his lips.

"Shall I drop you home? Your sister has given countless

missed calls from your number on my phone." Arjun said.

Ipsha realized that she had left her cell phone accidentally in her room.

She sighed, realizing that the beautiful moment has passed by and now it was time for her to return home.

On sensing Ipsha's unwillingness, Arjun cuddled her like a baby. Ipsha felt tranquil in his strong arms.

"Do you trust me, Ipsha?" Arjun whispered in her ear.

"Yes, Arjun. The truth in your eyes whispered to my heart how much you love me." Ipsha whispered back in Arjun's ears.

"We will meet tomorrow. If Akashi stops you, tell her the same thing that you told me just now." Arjun said.

It was 7 pm in the evening and Ipsha realized that she should go home. Running away from Akashi won't make the matter easier for her and Arjun. She should face it instead of running away from it. She hugged Arjun for ten minutes before leaving for her house.

BLANKET OF DARK CLOUDS

"Only when darkness is at its zenith, there is the probability of light to peep in again."

By the time Ipsha reached her house, she gathered courage to face Akashi. She was no longer the timid girl, scared of hiding things from her elder sister.

"Thank God! You are back. I was so worried." Akashi said after opening the door. She hugged her, but Ipsha did not respond.

"You cannot imagine how relieved I am now. I was so scared that the criminal might hurt you." Akashi said patting Ipsha's back as she hugged her. On the mention of the word criminal, Ipsha was infuriated. She released herself from Akashi's embrace and gave her a disapproving look.

"Stop it, Akashi. I love him. Please don't insult him in front of me by calling him a criminal."

"You might not be aware of his reality. He was running from the police, trust me. If you would have seen him that day at the railway station, you would have abhorred him. He looked just like a criminal with month old stubble and belligerent eyes. Now, he has done this makeover and given himself a polished look so that he can lure innocent people like you. Don't fall prey to his dangerous intentions, Ipsha." Akashi explained with patience.

"I know everything about Arjun. You only know the surface, whereas I know the entire thing. He had shared the entire story of his life with me. It takes a lot of courage to open up about the tragedies that one has seen in his childhood. Arjun is brave enough to tell me everything about his life without keeping any walls between us. So what if he is not the son of Akhilesh Walia! So what if he is the son of a poor security guard who was compelled to get involved in drug trafficking to save his family from financial problems! I love him more now because of his honesty. His love for me is true and unpretentious." Ipsha declared, startling Akashi.

Akashi was taken aback to see the fire in Ipsha's eyes with which she was defending Arjun. The word drug trafficking hit her mind and she became silent. Akashi was unsure in the morning about what Arjun could have left in her bag that day, but now she had a clue. She made a mental note to search her belongings meticulously for any clue that she can use against Arjun.

"Will you say something, now?" Ipsha asked in anger

"He is not the right person for you. Why can't you see that?"

"I don't care. I love him and he loves me too. It's all that matters to me."

"This is not love; this is self-destruction. All your friends were in school today and you were spending time with a person who has criminal records. He is chased by the police every other day. You are incapable of taking important decisions of your life because you are not even an adult." Akashi said.

"Stop it, Akashi."

"Arjun had doubts that he left something in my bag when he was chased by the police in the Howrah Station that day.

Therefore, he was stalking me since many days to find out if I know anything about him. He doesn't love you. He is here only for his illegal work." Akashi said, leaving Ipsha speechless. This piece of truth was unknown to Ipsha.

"What rubbish are you saying? Have you lost it? Arjun used to stalk me because he loves me." Ipsha shouted.

"He is a criminal, Ipsha. Such people are deceivers. They can never love anyone." Akashi said with patience.

"I won't bear a word against Arjun. Just leave me alone." Ipsha shouted and stormed into her room.

**

Ipsha did not have dinner. She talked to Arjun the entire night. She told him what Akashi said about his stalking.

"Akashi lied to you, Ipsha. If it was the truth, then she could have shown you the thing that I left in her bag for which I was stalking her. Well, I don't want to tell you, but I feel Akashi is attracted to me." Arjun said.

"What?"

"Yes. I felt so. Today, at dawn, she met me all alone in my hotel. She could have told you that she has doubts about me and wants to meet me. Moreover, telling you that I was stalking her points to the fact that she is interested in me." Arjun paused. There was silence for a minute after which Arjun spoke again "Perhaps, I am wrong."

"You can be right too. I don't know. Let's not talk about this." Ipsha said in a low voice.

"I love you, Ipsha. I saw a vacuum in your eyes. You camouflaged it with your effervescent laughter, but I noticed it. I wanted to answer the questions that were concealed beneath your laughter for a lifetime." Arjun said.

"I always felt lonely, Arjun. Akashi is the best sister anyone can ever get, but I always missed my parents. I always felt a void that was impossible to fill. Only with your arrival, I could feel the vacuum disappearing into nothingness. I started feeling happy." Ipsha confessed.

"I love you and I will never hurt you, Ipsha." Arjun said, sensing her love for him.

"I love you too, Arjun."

They decided to meet early in the morning at Delo, the topmost region of Kalimpong. Arjun was eager to try Paragliding and Ipsha couldn't help but comply with his wish.

Ipsha knew that she was madly in love with Arjun. She tried not to believe what Arjun said about Akashi's interest for him. She felt helpless for hurting Akashi.

Only time can do wonders. Not me.

She didn't realize when she fell asleep.

On the other hand, Akashi couldn't let even an ounce of sleep settle in her eyes. She knocked the door and requested Ipsha to have her dinner, but she did not listen. The distance between Ipsha and her was growing every day and it felt unbearable. She was clueless about how she could eradicate the growing distance between them.

The entire night went by, tossing and turning on the bed, as Akashi thought of a possible solution. All she could see in front of her was a blanket of darkness with no hope of light.

**

Do you realize?
How irrevocably you possess my mind
Distracting me time and again
Turning me crazy in your love, with every passing second?

Do you know?
How your thoughts cast a spell on me
Making me stay awake in the long nights
Tossing and turning till the sky is alight?

"You write so well. The lines are beautiful, Arjun." Ipsha said after reading the poem for the third time. Arjun handed her a small paper where he scribbled the poem, after reaching Delo.

"I mean every single word. I am not a poet. These are the ramblings of my heart to convey my feelings to you." Arjun said caressing Ipsha's cheek.

"Stop calling them ramblings. They sound magic to my ears." Ipsha said, cheerfully.

"What did Akashi say when you were getting out of the house?" Arjun asked with concern.

"She was about to give me a long lecture, but I stormed out of the house. Arjun, I feel bad because of the distance that has grown between her and me, but I cannot listen to her and cut all ties with you. I love you a lot." Ipsha said, looking at Arjun. He pulled her into his arms as he could clearly see how much she loves him.

"This. .the warmth of your arms is my paradise. I don't want to lose it ever." Ipsha said, snuggling into Arjun's arms. The place soon got crowded with enthusiastic tourists who wanted to try paragliding.

"I will be here in a minute." Arjun said and walked towards the counter.

Ipsha looked at the people around her. She saw a bulky woman arguing with her husband, who was unwilling to let her try paragliding.

"Jai, I read it on the internet. They have stated that people who weigh more than 100 kgs are not allowed to do it. I am only 80 kgs. Then what is the problem?" She asked her husband who looked very worried.

Ipsha smiled as she looked at the couple bickering with each other.

"Love is such a beautiful thing. Even the small fights look so pleasing." Ipsha said, pointing at the couple.

"Sweetheart, I will only and only love you. There will be no room for fights." Arjun said, pulling Ipsha's cheek.

Arjun and Ipsha climbed up the hill holding hands. Ipsha

realized that with every passing moment, she was falling more in love with Arjun.

"So, aren't you feeling nervous?" Ipsha asked Arjun.

"I have done a paragliding course two years back. I was in Pune for some work of Mr. Basu when I thought of fulfilling my dream of flying in the sky." Arjun winked at her. "So, today I am going to be your pilot," Arjun said, leaving Ipsha speechless.

"Really? I can't believe this. You are full of surprises, Arjun."

"I hope it's a good surprise and you can confide in me."

"I confide in you with my whole life."

"So, shall we fly now?"

Ipsha nodded with childlike enthusiasm. Arjun and Ipsha put on the belts around them. Although Ipsha told Arjun that she confides in him, there was a lingering fear in her heart.

"Arjun, I hope you are really an expert in paragliding." Ipsha said before Arjun was about to take off.

"Yes, my little girl. I will not let anything happen to you ever." Arjun assured Ipsha and took off the flight.

Arjun and Ipsha felt surreal. They were flying in the sky with each other, so many feet above the ground. They were living a dream.

"Oh! It feels so lovely Arjun. I feel that we are in a Utopian place. I wish we both were birds who could fly forever and no human being could have disturbed us." Ipsha said, feeling the wind on her face.

"No one can ever separate us, Ipsha. We will always be with each other." Arjun said. Ipsha closed her eyes and felt blessed to have Arjun in her life.

They flew for about fifteen minutes in the sky, going from here to there, doing waltz with the wind. The wind, the sky and their love were doing a merry jig, without any inhibitions.

After what seemed like an eternity, Arjun landed with Ipsha. After they took off the helmet, belts and apparatus from their body, Ipsha embraced Arjun tightly. Tears of happiness were streaming down her eyes.

"This was heavenly. Thank you for this amazing gift." Ipsha said, wrapping her arms around Arjun. Arjun kissed her forehead. They sat on the grass and talked to each other. They enjoyed watching the colorful paragliders in the sky.

During the time of sundown, the place became isolated. Ipsha and Arjun could still not get enough of each other. They whispered sweet nothings, cracked jokes and laughed their heart out.

Right at that time, when everything was rosy, a blanket of dark clouds engulfed them. Ipsha noticed three tall, muscular men with unpolished faces walking towards them, looking at Arjun with wrath.

The color drained from Arjun's face as he saw the men approaching towards them.

"Look guys, this is not the place to discuss things. Come to my hotel, we will talk peacefully there." Arjun said, getting up frantically. Ipsha looked puzzled and frightened with the course of events.

"Ha! You want to sing and dance with your girlfriend in the hills now. Let us also be a part of the show." One man said with sarcasm.

"Ipsha, you go to your house now." Arjun said looking at Ipsha.

"Who are they, Arjun? I won't leave you at any cost. Let us both go from here now." Ipsha suggested.

Arjun tried to convince Ipsha, but to no avail. The dark clouds became darker with every passing second.

IN TROUBLED WATERS

"Life is a constant struggle of making choices at every turn of the road and doubting the next second if the choice made was right."

Akashi's neighbor informed her that some serious commotion took place in Delo. By eavesdropping Ipsha's conversation with Arjun, Akashi knew that they met at Delo to try paragliding. The news that her neighbor brought shook her completely. She immediately went outside to search Ipsha. She reached Delo and found a couple of policemen examining the place. A crowd of local people was also gathered there.

"Sir, what has happened here?" Akashi asked a cop, mustering some amount of courage. Her heart beats raced as she asked the question.

"Are you the daughter of D'Souza Sir?" The policeman asked, recognizing Akashi at once.

Akashi nodded.

"I was his student." The policeman said with a smile. Akashi felt relieved and smiled back. She thought to derive some information from the policeman.

"It's really deplorable that a small town like Kalimpong is getting untidy with criminals and convicts. A few people, involved in illegal activities got into a dirty squabble here this evening. We arrested two of them and learned that they are involved in drug trafficking." The policeman explained.

Akashi shivered as she heard the news.

Did police arrest Arjun? Where is Ipsha? Should I ask him about my sister? Perhaps, I should. It's 8pm and this is the only way I can get some clue of where Ipsha is right now.

The policeman pointed at the left side and said, "We have arrested those two people, whereas the other two have fled."

Akashi noticed the two people who were handcuffed. Arjun was not one of them. After thinking for a minute, Akashi rushed towards her house.

She found that Ipsha was in her room. Akashi felt relieved and thanked her stars. She asked Ipsha to open the door, but to her surprise, Ipsha did not listen.

"Are you fine, Ipsha? Tell me all that had happened there. Where is Arjun?" Akashi asked from the other side of the door.

"It's been a dangerous day. Arjun is safe." Ipsha replied bluntly.

"Where is Arjun? The police are looking for him. I hope you know that." Akashi further asked.

"He is safe. Now, let me sleep. I will talk to you tomorrow. Please." Ipsha said with exhaustion.

Akashi felt befuddled with Ipsha's behavior. She asked Malati Masi if she has seen Ipsha entering the house, but to her sheer disappointment, she said no.

"I was at our neighbor's place. During that time, Ipsha must have entered the house."

A wave of uncertainty somersaulted in Akashi's mind. She felt helpless and wanted to talk to Ipsha desperately.

She finally decided to wait for the morning. She wanted

to give Ipsha some time to get over the unpleasant incident that she witnessed in the evening. However, peace eluded her when she heard Ipsha talking to someone at night.

When she eavesdropped, she could understand that Ipsha was talking to Arjun.

She must be talking over the phone. I am worrying unnecessarily.

Akashi pacified herself and went to sleep.

**

If the last evening was a thunderstorm, the morning arrived with the promise of a devastating hurricane.

Arjun Sharma, who was staying in the Elgin Silver Oaks Hotel under the identity of Arjun Walia, the son of businessman Akhilesh Walia is missing. Police have discovered several boxes of cocaine, heroin, and other drugs from his room. It is found that he is working as a drug trafficker under some influential man of Kolkata. Last night at Delo, there was an ugly fight between Arjun and another group of drug traffickers. Arjun and another man fled when police reached the place. The investigation is on and the police are trying to get to the root of the case. This is the first time a beautiful place like Kalimpong is witnessing such a deplorable incident.

The morning news shocked Akashi.

If Arjun is not in his hotel, then where is he?

Akashi knocked Ipsha's room and after some time, Ipsha came out of the room.

The news flashed every few minutes and Ipsha had no other choice than listening to it.

"What had exactly happened yesterday?" Akashi asked.

"Exactly what they are showing in the news," Ipsha said nonchalantly, biting an apple.

"Fine! Where is Arjun?"

After a silence of five minutes, Ipsha shocked Akashi by saying, "With me."

"What? You mean in our house?" Akashi shrieked and Ipsha gave a grimace.

"I had no other place to bring Arjun. Please understand that he is in danger. Police will shoot him. He will die and I can't let him die. How can I?" Ipsha screamed and was on the verge of tears. Akashi was taken aback by Ipsha's volatile reaction.

The incident of last evening must have shaken her up.

"Why didn't you tell Arjun to stay in our guest room?" Akashi said.

"I can't take risks. You are a shrewd woman. You can inform the police and take Arjun away from me. Then the police will kill him ruthlessly in front of my eyes and you will get happiness. Won't you?" Ipsha shouted. Her eyes were glistening with tears.

Akashi did not react to Ipsha's words. She could fathom how scared and shaken Ipsha was. Therefore, she let those words roll down her back.

"Police will surely find Arjun one day or the other. Kalimpong is such a small place. It's not that difficult to find someone. And my dear, why will police kill Arjun? He will only be arrested and then the powerful person, under whom he works, will bail him out of the jail. Trust me." Akashi said with a smile.

"No, they will kill him. Are you saying that we should hand over Arjun to the police?" Ipsha screamed at Akashi.

"I am saying that Arjun should surrender to the police. That will be the best thing. Let me talk to Arjun once." As Akashi said the last few words, Ipsha looked at her in anger.

"I won't let you do this. If you love me, then you will let Arjun stay here. Else I will hurt myself. Police can't find him." Ipsha said and rushed towards her room. She closed the door loudly, leaving Akashi flustered.

Akashi wondered what she should do in this situation.

The news flashing the details of Arjun every few minutes

made her feel sick. Ipsha came out of her room only once and took her lunch. She took enough rice for two people. Akashi tried to talk to her, but Ipsha did not care to listen.

People in Kalimpong respected Akashi's father. It is because of her father that most people in Kalimpong knew and loved them. Akashi winced as she thought her father's name will be tainted if the police found out that they are hiding a criminal in their house.

After lunch, Akashi decided to call the police and tell them that Arjun is in their house. She thought that by doing so, she would be able to save Ipsha from the dangerous man. But Ipsha's warning of hurting herself worked as a hindrance. Akashi found herself in troubled waters. She couldn't let things be. At the same time, she did not know what would be the perfect step at this crucial hour.

Akashi did not realize when it was 9 pm. She was sitting like a statue on the sofa since afternoon. She completely lost track of time. As she neared Ipsha's room, she could hear whispers. It was evident that Ipsha was talking to Arjun.

Finally, Akashi decided to talk to Arjun. She wanted to explain Arjun that he was bringing a mammoth danger for Ipsha by taking help from her. Akashi realized that only Arjun can save them from this situation.

THE CATASTROPHE

"Within a few seconds, everything can change in our lives either in the form of a miracle or a catastrophe. Life is unpredictable beyond our comprehension."

Akashi was about to knock the door when the bell of the house rang. She wondered who could have visited them at this hour of the night. With an anxious face, Akashi opened the door. She was shocked to find two policemen standing in front of her. For a few seconds, she felt so giddy that she thought she will faint.

"Yes, Sir," Akashi managed to speak after collecting her composure.

"We have got the information that your younger sister, Ipsha was a very good friend of Arjun. Therefore, we doubt that Arjun can hide in this house. We have come to search for Arjun and to talk to Ipsha." One policeman explained.

Sweat beads appeared on her forehead and she did not know what she should say.

"Which is Ipsha's room?" The policemen enquired. Akashi pointed her finger in the direction of Ipsha's room without uttering any word. She was too shocked to think.

115

The policemen knocked the door of Ipsha's room for about five minutes, but no response came from inside.

"Is your sister alright?" One policeman asked Akashi.

"Actually, no. She is not keeping well. She is sleeping. Arjun is not here, Sir. I request you to talk to Ipsha some other day." Akashi pleaded.

"In this entire town of Kalimpong, Arjun was extremely close to your sister. They have been spotted together in several places. In fact, the day Arjun went missing, your sister was there with him. We cannot treat the matter casually. If your sister doesn't open the door, then we will be forced to break open the door." The police officer said sternly.

Akashi was taken aback by the response. She was concerned about Ipsha's safety more than anything else.

"Ipsha, please open the door. If you don't open it, the police will be compelled to break open the door. Please, open the door dear." Akashi said, knocking the door.

After a few minutes, Ipsha opened the door with swollen eyes and unkempt hair. She looked angry and hurt. The police officers entered her room and started searching everywhere. They couldn't find Arjun, but they noticed that Ipsha's window was wide open.

"Was Arjun here all the while?" The police officers asked Ipsha.

"Sir, you have searched her room. Arjun is nowhere. Why are you asking such a question to her? My sister is not keeping well. I request you earnestly to leave her on her own." Akashi intervened.

"Here, this is Arjun's jacket. What is it doing in Miss Ipsha's room?" A police officer asked pointing at the jacket.

Akashi searched words in the air, but to no avail. She looked at Ipsha who was quiet.

"Sir, I don't have any idea. As you can see, my sister is not well. Can you please investigate tomorrow? She needs to sleep." Akashi said, mustering some amount of courage.

"We also need to check the other rooms of the house, Miss Akashi." The police officers said and started searching every nook and corner of the house.

"Alright. Tomorrow morning, we will be here again. If we find out that you were sheltering a criminal after seeing the news on TV, you both will be severely punished." The policeman said and left.

Akashi felt sick with the sequence of events. The ground beneath her seemed to move away and she tried to find an anchor. She moved towards Ipsha's room. Ipsha was sitting stoically on her bed, holding Arjun's jacket on her lap. She sat beside Ipsha.

"Everything will be fine." Akashi said embracing Ipsha.

Ipsha outrageously jerked Akashi's hands off her and looked at her in anger.

"Such a chameleon you are! You called the police to separate Arjun from me and now you are putting this act as if you have done nothing." Ipsha screamed.

"What are you talking about? How can you even imagine that I can call the police?" Akashi asked. Out of all the unpredictable incidents of the day, this was like a bolt from the blue.

"You were against Arjun hiding in my room, right from the moment I told you. It's so easy to understand that you have called the police, else they wouldn't have got a clue." Ipsha screamed. Malati Masi tried to console her, but she was too aggressive to listen to anyone.

"Yes, I was against him hiding in your room and so I wanted to talk to him. But before I could do that, the police came. I did not call the police. Trust me." Akashi tried to explain.

"You are not my sister. You are my enemy." Ipsha started crying, covering her face with Arjun's jacket.

"No, dearest. I have no one in the world other than you. Don't say such words. They hurt. Tell me where Arjun is. We both will help him out." Akashi said with tears crawling down her cheeks. Ipsha's venomous words were too much for her to swallow.

"You want to know where Arjun is and hand him over to the police, don't you?" Ipsha shouted, amid her sobs.

"No, Ipsha. I want to help Arjun for your sake." Akashi replied, exhausted.

"I don't know where Arjun is right now. He managed to escape from that window when the police were knocking the door. He said that he would call me when he will get an opportunity." Ipsha said, looking at the direction of the window.

Akashi swallowed the information and looked at Ipsha's face without speaking a word.

"Why did you do this with me? What if the police kill my Arjun? What if I can't see him any day?" Ipsha screamed after a silence of two minutes.

"Nothing like that will happen." Akashi said, unable to fathom how she can pacify her sister.

"I don't feel like staying in this house. I should rather see where Arjun is." Ipsha said and rushed towards the living room.

"Ipsha, please stop. It is 10 pm. Where will you find Arjun? We will search him tomorrow morning. Wait for some time. He might call you soon." Akashi said following Ipsha.

"And what if the police shoot him tonight? What if my Arjun gets killed in police encounter? How will I live without him? Why have you done such a pathetic thing with me, Akashi? " Ipsha started screaming again, her eyes filled with tears.

"Please relax, my dear. Nothing like that will happen." Akashi tried to pacify Ipsha when she grabbed the fruit knife from the table.

"What are you trying to do, Ipsha? Keep the knife down.

We both will find Arjun. I know some police officers who will help us. Put it down." Akashi panicked.

"No, I don't want to live without Arjun. I know you are totally against our relationship. You will try your level best to separate Arjun from me. And you are already successful in your mission, my dearest elder sister. You party at your accomplishment as I quit this battle." Ipsha said the last words with a sarcastic smile.

"Ipsha, stop this nonsense." Akashi approached Ipsha to take the knife from her hand but it was too late. Ipsha had slit her wrist. A jet of fresh blood oozed out from her wrist. Within a few seconds, Ipsha fell on the floor, unconscious.

Everything went still for a few seconds. Akashi's mind stopped working. She felt she is in the middle of a cursed nightmare. She got back her senses when Malati Masi shook her from her blackout state. Finally, it registered in Akashi's mind that every bit of it is a part of reality.

"Ipsha Ipsha! Somebody help!" Akashi howled at the sight of her sister lying amidst a pool of blood.

AFTERMATH

"God never closes a door without opening another. The promise of light and the hope of a better tomorrow always surround us, even in the darkest phase of our life."

It was an abhorrent sight. Blood swept down from the slit of the wrist, turning the shirt and the sheet of the hospital bed crimson. The nurses yelled out for doctors for attending the patient at 10 pm in the thunderous night.

Akashi took a long sigh to ebb down the jitters running down her spine. She saw her sister, Ipsha lying unconscious on the hospital bed with no doctors to attend her.

"When will a doctor attend my sister?" Akashi asked with trembling lips to the nurse who glanced at her with disgust.

"So, the girl who has slit her wrist is your younger sister. Such a young girl committing suicide! " The nurse blurted out the words rubbing salt in Akashi's fresh wounds.

"Doctor Sharma will be here within some time. Wait." The nurse said after scanning Akashi from top to bottom.

Akashi sat on the wooden bench outside the room where Ipsha has been laid. She said a silent prayer for her sister, who is the only person she has in this vast world. The sound of the thunder interrupted her prayer and made her feel uneasy. Right then, a nurse summoned her, who unlike the previous one had kind eyes and a thin smile.

"Doctor Sharma is attending your sister. He has told you to sit in his cabin as he wants to talk to you about your sister." The nurse said and gave Akashi the directions to Dr. Sharma's cabin.

As every minute ticked past in the clock, Akashi's patience wore off, sitting in the cabin. She remembered the absolute berserk way in which Ipsha behaved before she slit her wrist with the fruit knife. Akashi dug her nails on her skin as she recalled Ipsha's tears and her screams calling out 'Arjun'.

"Hello, this is Dr. Sharma." Akashi's disturbing thoughts got faded by the doctor's voice. She looked at him blankly, fearing to hear the worst.

"It's a fortune that Ipsha is safe now. If the slit was a few centimeters below, it would be perhaps difficult to save her. I have injected her sleeping drug because she needs a deep sleep." The doctor smiled at Akashi after completing his words. Akashi mumbled a meek thank you and covered her face with her hands as she realized she could have lost Ipsha.

"Why did she slit her wrist?" The doctor asked the question which was inevitable yet excruciating.

Akashi looked at the doctor with tear-stained eyes. His kind and affable face calmed her to some extent. She looked through the window and noticed that the rain had stopped and so had the thunder. The sky was quite tranquil; the clock read midnight. The beautiful landscapes of Kalimpong were concealed in the blanket of darkness. Dr. Sharma kept looking at Akashi as she studied her surroundings.

"I know being an elder sister, it hurts to talk about the reason behind your sister's attempt at suicide. But I need to know the reason as I am her doctor. I hope not, but if Ipsha

121

again attempts suicide after regaining her senses, we can't help unless we know what's wrong with her." The doctor explained.

"I don't know where I should begin. Everything seems so strange to me now. I still can't understand why she took such a desperate step." Akashi winced.

"Tell me the entire thing so that I get a clear picture. It's midnight now. My duty is until 6 am in the morning. We have enough time." Dr. Sharma proposed.

"Trust me. It's only for Ipsha's well-being." Dr. Sharma said in a convincing tone. Akashi looked through the window with a heavy heart as she realized that she has to share so much about her and Ipsha's life to a stranger. She didn't want the doctor to judge Ipsha or her, but she had no options.

"Don't over think. I assure you that it's only for Ipsha's treatment and well-being. There is a saying that you should never hide anything from doctors and lawyers. Unless they know the entire truth, they cannot help you." The doctor repeated until Akashi started speaking.

**

Akashi went into the hospital room where Ipsha was sleeping peacefully. Ipsha's left hand was bandaged. Although the dawn had arrived with the promise of morning, Akashi could fathom that the morning would be devoid of sunlight.

It was still raining and a distasteful gloomy aura filled the hospital room. Akashi quietly sat on the chair beside Ipsha's bed and gazed at Ipsha. Beads of tears appeared in her eyes as she looked at her sister.

Why have you done this, my love? Why have you punished me in this manner?

Akashi wondered where Arjun could be at that moment. She was sure that as Ipsha would regain her senses, she would ask for Arjun. The doctor told her to keep Ipsha happy and distracted so that suicidal thoughts don't greet her again.

Apparently, Ipsha is suffering from shock and stress that has prevented her from using logic. She is over emotional and her mind is not working properly. She needs time to heal and most of all, she needs Arjun.

How can I find Arjun? Even if I find him, how will Arjun stay with Ipsha? The police are chasing him.

Akashi felt disturbed by the questions that were hitting her mind. She was lonely and clueless. She could not discuss such things with her neighbors. She needed someone whom she could trust with all her heart, with whom she could share her burden. She needed someone to confide in and someone who would lend her a compassionate ear.

Her fingers magically dialed a number.

"Hello!" A sleepy voice greeted her on the other side of the phone. Akashi looked at her watch which read 5.30 am.

I shouldn't have called Vihaan at this hour.

Akashi was about to disconnect the phone when Vihaan spoke.

"Akashi! Are you fine?"

"I am in a terrible state. Ipsha has committed suicide. I am in the hospital." Akashi whispered so that Ipsha's slumber doesn't get disturbed.

"What are you talking? How did this happen?" Vihaan shrieked from the other end of the phone. He couldn't believe the shocking information that he received at the crack of dawn.

"It's a long story, Vihaan." Akashi managed to say as tears rolled down her cheeks. Vihaan's caring voice opened the lid of the bottle where she had suppressed her emotions for a long time. Akashi's tears became copious with every passing second.

"I know, dear. It's not possible to explain everything over the phone." Vihaan said.

"I feel so lonely. I cannot take this on my shoulders, all

alone." Akashi said amid her tears.

"I will be there within two days. Till then, you take care of Ipsha and yourself." Vihaan said promptly without thinking anything.

"Really?" Akashi said, surprised.

"I care for you and Ipsha. See you soon. I will text you."

Vihaan's words were like a ray of sunshine in the gloomy morning. Akashi needed him by her side. She was tired of fighting it all alone.

Akashi went near Ipsha and caressed her cheeks gently. She whispered:

Get well soon, darling. You are my life. You are the only flower in my barren garden. I won't let anything happen to you.

THE CLOUDS OF MONSOON

"If rainwater percolates through the walls of a room, the beauty of monsoon gets lost at once. Circumstances determine whether the monsoon is romantic or melancholic."

"Miss Akashi, your sister is doing well. She has regained consciousness." Dr. Sharma said in a cheerful demeanor, which broke Akashi's nap.

Sitting on the wooden bench outside Doctor Sharma's cabin, Akashi didn't realize when she fell asleep.

"Thank God. How is Ipsha now?" Akashi said with a sigh of relief. The news made her feel better.

"She is weak and depressed. I have prescribed some blood tests which need to be done at the earliest. She had lost plenty of blood. I insist you keep her in the hospital for at least two more days. Moreover, her state of mind is not good. She is depressed and therefore, she needs supervision all day and night. She might get suicidal thoughts again at home."

"Did she say anything after waking up?" Akashi asked with a sullen face.

125

"She is unbelievably quiet. I told her that I am her doctor. I said that you are right outside, waiting for her to wake up. I also asked her if she is feeling better and that she will soon be discharged from the hospital. But she did not reply." Doctor Sharma shook his head.

"What should I do, doctor?" Akashi asked.

"Ipsha needs love and attention. She is going through a trauma. She is only seventeen and the events of the last few days were too heavy for her tender heart. You need to be patient. Try to make her feel that you are with her and that everything is going to be fine. Even if she yells at you, don't react. Be calm and make sure that she sleeps well. A good night's sleep will help Ipsha to recover better." The doctor explained and Akashi nodded.

Akashi felt uneasy to meet Ipsha. Those bloodshot eyes and screams right before Ipsha had slit her wrist came running in front of her eyes. It was still raining and thundering. The clouds of monsoon mirrored the monsoon in her life.

Before walking into Ipsha's room, she promised to stay calm and hold her composure.

Even if Ipsha yells or shouts, I won't react and say a word against Arjun. God, please give me the strength!

Akashi smiled as she entered the room. Ipsha looked at Akashi and then turned her face away.

"How are you feeling now?" Akashi asked, running her fingers through Ipsha's hair.

There was no reply. The silence gnawed its teeth at Akashi, but she did not lose her patience.

"Ipsha, do you want to have something?"

Silence prevailed in the gloomy hospital room.

"I know you have slit your wrist in anger, but you should have at least thought about Arjun. Will he like to see you in this condition?" Akashi deliberately mentioned Arjun's name so that Ipsha speaks.

She stepped in the right direction. Ipsha's eyes surrendered to the tears that were locked inside her eyes. After a few seconds, she wiped off her tears and looked at Akashi helplessly.

"Where is my phone?" Ipsha asked.

"It's in your room, most probably. Since yesterday, you are in the hospital." Akashi explained.

"Oh no! Arjun might have called me. Please get me my phone as soon as possible." Ipsha started panicking.

"Calm down, Ipsha. You have already lost a lot of blood. The doctor has prescribed numerous tests for you."

"I can't calm down. Stop being pretentious! I am in this hospital because of you…because you called the police. Now please, get me my phone." Ipsha started screaming.

"Okay. I am telling Malati Masi to bring your phone as soon as possible." Akashi said which calmed Ipsha to some extent.

Akashi dialed the landline of their house and told Malati Masi to bring Ipsha's phone to the hospital. There was an awkward silence between the two sisters. After a few minutes, Ipsha spoke.

"Arjun did not want to leave me and go, but I insisted him to sneak out of the window when I realized that the police have come to chase him…

He was worried about me…his eyes were filled with tears…And then he went out and within a few seconds, disappeared in the darkness…

He did not want to come to my house…I dragged him as I thought he would be safe with me. Why did you betray me, Akashi? You destroyed everything." Ipsha started sobbing.

Ipsha's sobs broke Akashi's heart. She did not realize that Ipsha was so much attached to Arjun. She disregarded it as some puppy love, unable to fathom that it was something intense.

"I did not call the police. Yes, I thought for a moment,

127

but…" Akashi's words were cut short by Ipsha's rage.

"So, you admit it. You thought to call the police and separate Arjun from me. How insensitive and selfish a person you are!" Ipsha threw the glass kept on the table beside her bed, startling Akashi.

The nurses came running to Ipsha's room, after hearing the shrill sound of the glass on the floor.

"Tell this woman to get out of my room or else I will hurt myself." Ipsha shouted in front of the nurses who looked flabbergasted. Akashi went out of the room without saying a word as she did not want to create a scene.

As she stood outside, she saw Malati Masi running towards her with an apprehensive face.

"Is Ipsha better now?" She asked Akashi.

Akashi nodded and took Ipsha's phone from Malati Masi's hand. Before handing over the phone to Ipsha, Akashi thought of checking the call list to see if Arjun had called her. But to her disappointment, the phone was locked. There were 5 missed calls, but Akashi couldn't check the number as the phone required a password.

Akashi told one of the nurses to hand over the phone to Ipsha.

"Ipsha is better now. You come home and take some rest." Malati Masi said to Akashi.

Akashi realized that there was no use of staying at the hospital. She agreed with Malati Masi but decided to meet Ipsha before leaving.

Ipsha was over the phone, crying and smiling at the same time. Akashi realized at once that she was talking to Arjun.

"Please meet me soon, Arjun. I hate staying in this hospital, which looks like a jail. I am missing you terribly."

Akashi came out of the room without disturbing Ipsha. With a retired gait, she proceeded towards her home with Malati Masi. On reaching home, she sat on the couch and started weeping, looking at the photograph of her parents.

Malati Masi told her that she is strong enough to tackle all the adversities that life throws her way. Akashi had some amount of rice on Malati Masi's insistence. It was after almost 24 hours she had some food. She survived those excruciating hours only on coffee.

After finishing her dinner, something clicked Akashi's mind. She rushed inside Ipsha's room and looked for Arjun's jacket. She spotted Arjun's jacket and started examining it. She found his wallet, sunglass and a small notepad inside the jacket. There were around 5000 rupees in his wallet and the last page of the notepad had Ipsha's name written in red ink.

Arjun had to rush when the police came. So he forgot to take his wallet.

As Akashi searched for other belongings of Arjun in Ipsha's room, she saw a pile of sketches. On examining the sketches, she could understand that they were sketches of Arjun and Ipsha. It seemed that Ipsha had written her love story through those sketches.

Akashi felt too tired to study each sketch right then. She carried the pile of papers to her room and retired to sleep. She was too weary to think anything that night.

FINALLY SOME HOPE

"There lies a mirror of hope amid our pain, where we can see the reflection of the person we love the most. One word or caress from that person can heal us even in our worst days."

"I want my drawing book," Ipsha said to Akashi when she was feeding her soup in the hospital.

"Ipsha, you are too weak. Your hand is bandaged. After you get well, paint and sketch to your heart's content."

Ipsha frowned.

"My left hand is injured, Akashi. I draw with my right hand. I want my drawing book, pencils, eraser and paints here, right now."

"Why have you become so stubborn? You wanted your phone; I gave it to you yesterday. But painting with such a weak body is not right." Akashi explained.

"I am not stubborn. If I seriously was, then I would have never talked to you. But Arjun told me that you are my sister and that I should not misbehave with you." Ipsha said with a frown.

"How is Arjun now? Did you tell him that the police are

looking for him?" Akashi asked with a little curiosity.

"Yes, he knows."

"Is he still in Kalimpong?"

"Do you think I am a fool? If I share with you, you might give the information to the police." Ipsha said with a scornful look.

"Oh dear! I don't intend to do any such thing." Akashi felt too tired to explain.

"You can leave now. Arjun can call me anytime and I don't want you to listen to our conversation. Please bring the things I asked for." Ipsha said and got busy with her phone. Akashi had no other option other than walking out of the room.

She started crying as soon as she reached the vacant corridor. Ipsha's bitter words were stinging her. It was getting difficult for her to battle the tempest day after day.

Right then, when she was fighting with her vulnerability, she felt a loving touch on her shoulder.

"Akashi!" She recognized the voice and touch at once. It was the voice that she wanted to hear from the core of her heart.

She turned around and saw Vihaan standing in front of her. Vihaan took her in his arms.

"Everything will be fine, my dear. Ipsha will recover soon. Trust me. I am with you." Vihaan said.

Only Akashi knew what this loving hug, these caring words and this support meant for her. She buried her face in Vihaan's chest and cried to her heart's content. She was tired of crying alone in her room with the pillow as her only companion.

Vihaan realized how much Akashi must have needed him in the dark hours. He felt pathetic for breaking up with her. He wondered why he did that stupid and ridiculous thing on Akashi's birthday.

He thought he was incapable of maintaining the long

distance relationship. So, the only solution he had was breaking up.

How ludicrous it was of me! I should have tried to work it out instead of breaking up.

"Are you okay?" Vihaan asked.

"Feeling much better. Thank you so much for being here." Akashi said, breaking the embrace. Her smile calmed his heart. He was glad that he could convert her tears into a faint smile.

"Don't dare to be formal with me." Vihaan said.

"Alright. I need to bring some things from home for Ipsha. Will you come along?" Akashi asked Vihaan.

"After you, my girl." Vihaan said with a smile.

Akashi smiled back.

**

Akashi stuffed the jute bag with Ipsha's drawing book, pencils, paints, erasers, palette and brushes. She came out of Ipsha's room with the huge jute bag.

"Let's go to the hospital. I am done." Akashi declared.

"First, you tell me all that had happened in the last few days. I want to know what the matter is. I am pretty sure that you are also dying to share everything with me." Vihaan said, signaling Akashi to sit on the couch.

"You are right, Vihaan. All these things happened in a flash. I could not comprehend the darkness that Ipsha and I were walking into. It seems like a never ending nightmare." Akashi said sitting on the couch.

"Tell me all." Vihaan insisted. Akashi narrated the incidents that took place after he left Kalimpong.

Vihaan listened to her patiently, without interrupting her. When Akashi completed, he could see her gasping for breath. He held her hands.

"Relax, Akashi. What's done cannot be undone. This Arjun seems lunatic, doesn't he? I mean he started stalking you as he doubted that he left something in your bag. Then, all of a sudden, he fell in love with Ipsha and started stalking her. He tried to woo her in such weird ways by sending love notes and playing the harmonica.

After that, he lied to her about his identity. Then, after some days, he told the truth to her confidently that he is a drug trafficker. He stayed in her room when the police were chasing him and then he managed to escape too. This person sounds crazy, fake and counterfeit." Vihaan said with crooked eyebrows, as he tried to analyze the situation.

"Yeah, I agree with you. Arjun is a weird person. I don't know how Ipsha fell in this dungeon." Akashi said.

"Ipsha is a teenager who craves love and romance, like the romance shown in movies. So, she got attracted to the mystery surrounding Arjun." Vihaan said.

"You are right. I objected to their affair from the very beginning. That made her resent me." Akashi reasoned.

"Exactly. She believes you have separated Arjun from her. So she will keep things about Arjun under wraps." Vihaan said.

"I need to know where Arjun is right now. The police are searching him and they are after my life too. The police believe that I have given shelter to that criminal." Akashi panicked.

"I want to meet Ipsha. Let me see if I can do something." Vihaan said which provided a ray of hope to Akashi.

**

"Hello, Ipsha! How are you?" Vihaan said as he walked into the hospital room.

Ipsha looked at Vihaan and said that she was better. Akashi stood behind Vihaan with a large bag. Ipsha gave a reluctant smile to Vihaan and turned her face away. Akashi kept the drawing book, paints and pencils on the table beside Ipsha's bed. She left the room without saying a word. Vihaan sat on the chair and initiated the conversation.

133

"I know the entire thing. Trust me, I am against Akashi in this regard."

As the words of Vihaan reached Ipsha's ears, she looked at him.

"What do you mean?" Ipsha asked.

"I mean Akashi should have supported you and Arjun. I know she cares a lot for you, but she shouldn't have come between you and Arjun. If her support would have been strong, Arjun wouldn't have to flee away." Vihaan said with sincerity.

"I never expected you to support me, Vihaan." Ipsha said, confused.

"Your sister is conservative. I am quite liberal and so, I support you." Vihaan justified.

"Thank you so much, Vihaan. I am glad. Hey, wait Arjun is calling." Ipsha said looking at her phone.

Vihaan nodded and listened to Ipsha's conversation with Arjun.

They talked for a few minutes and then Ipsha disconnected the phone. The conversation was short. Ipsha told Arjun to take care and to meet her soon. Before disconnecting the call, Ipsha said that she understands him.

"You look sad," Vihaan said after Ipsha disconnected the phone.

"I want to meet Arjun," Ipsha said, helplessly.

"I can understand. Where is Arjun, now?" Vihaan asked in a cool demeanor.

"He is in Kalimpong but I don't know exactly where he is. He is just running away from the police." Ipsha said. Vihaan was satisfied that he could extract the information that he wanted to know.

"I am feeling sleepy, Vihaan. These medicines make me feel sleepy all the time. Do you mind if I sleep now?" Ipsha asked.

"Go to sleep, dear. I am here. I will leave after you fall

asleep." Vihaan said and covered Ipsha till her shoulders with the blanket. She dozed off within two minutes. Vihaan thought to check her phone to extract some information about Arjun.

He found that the phone was locked and demanded a password. Vihaan guessed and typed a few passwords, but the phone said incorrect password each time. After thinking for a few seconds, he typed *ipshalovesarjun*. He was delighted when the phone got unlocked.

Vihaan went to the message folder. There were no messages of Arjun. He then went to the calling list and to his surprise, saw that there were no incoming calls from Arjun. There were only outgoing calls which did not even last a minute.

Then, with whom did Ipsha talk before dozing off? Did she delete the recent call list? I was sitting here all the while. I didn't see her deleting anything on her phone.

Vihaan felt bizarre and dialed Arjun's number. All he could hear was that the number was unreachable.

The Fog

"Half-truth is like the zone between life and death. It is itching, frustrating and something that kills our sanity. It is better to stay under the canopy of a lie than to see the half-truth."

Akashi was sitting in the empty cafeteria of the hospital when Vihaan came running to her. He looked worried and out of place. Akashi was surprised to find him in that condition. She had never seen Vihaan so stressed about anything. He had always been the person who kept cool even in the most disturbing of circumstances.

"Is Ipsha alright?" Akashi asked, fearing the worst.

"She is sleeping." Vihaan managed to say.

"I got scared. What makes you look so worried?"

Vihaan grabbed a chair and sat down beside Akashi. He found it difficult to align his thoughts.

"There is much more to it than what meets the eye, Akashi." He finally said.

"Are you talking about Arjun?"

"I am talking about both Ipsha and Arjun," Vihaan said. He explained Akashi about the things that he found out from

136

Ipsha's phone a few minutes back.

"Perhaps, Arjun had switched off his phone after talking to Ipsha. Moreover, Ipsha is too clever. She must have deleted the recent call list." Akashi said.

"You are not getting me, Akashi. Ipsha talked for five minutes with Arjun in front of me. But when I checked her recent call list, the outgoing call did not last even a minute. It implies that the phone got disconnected as Arjun's number was unavailable. Are you getting me now, eh?" Vihaan became impatient as he tried to explain Akashi.

"Then, with whom was Ipsha talking in front of you for five minutes?" Akashi asked as Vihaan's explanation registered in her mind.

"This is what I am wondering." Vihaan replied.

"I think you did some mistake while checking the call list. You are tired Vihaan after the long journey. You should take rest." Akashi reasoned.

"God damn, Akashi! You feel that my mind is playing games with me." Vihaan shouted.

"I didn't mean that, Vihaan. I could not get any possible explanation other than this. I am already so much worried about losing Ipsha that…" Akashi broke down.

Vihaan felt terrible. Akashi was already battling with countless problems since the last few days and shouting on her was too insensitive of him. He took Akashi's hand in his.

"I am sorry. You are right. Ipsha might have deleted the calling list before dozing off. I am over thinking." Vihaan assured Akashi, but deep down he knew that things were not what it seems. But for the time being, he did not want to enhance Akashi's stress. He wanted to analyze the matter and then share with Akashi when he had a logical explanation.

Akashi leaned towards Vihaan and rested her head on his chest. She felt peaceful in Vihaan's presence. Vihaan wrapped his arm around her and they sat silently in the empty cafeteria for a while.

Vihaan noticed a police inspector approaching towards them. Akashi's eyes were closed as she rested her head on Vihaan's chest.

"Akashi?" Vihaan whispered in her ears.

Akashi opened her eyes and felt disturbed on noticing the police. Vihaan held her hand tight to assure her that he is with her.

"Hello, Miss D'Souza! How is your sister doing?" The inspector asked Akashi.

"She is better." Akashi said. She was scared that the police will ask about Arjun and accuse her of not revealing his whereabouts.

"Good to know that she is getting better." The inspector said with a smile and asked the owner of the cafeteria to bring three cups of tea.

The inspector sat in the cafeteria and sipped his tea. Akashi and Vihaan waited for him to speak. An air of uncertainty prevailed in the cafeteria. Akashi and Vihaan looked at each other from time to time with an unsure look.

"Now, I have come here to reveal the information that we have got about Arjun." The inspector finally said.

"Is Arjun arrested?" Akashi asked without being able to conceal her curiosity.

"Arjun is no more, Miss D'Souza." The inspector revealed.

"What?" Akashi shrieked but Vihaan was quiet. He was trying to figure out certain things, all at a time.

"Yes, we discovered his body last night." The inspector said.

"But right now Vihaan saw Ipsha talking to Arjun over the phone. Just a few minutes back." Akashi fumbled. She looked at Vihaan and asked, "Right? Then how is this possible?"

"Here, have some water. You need to calm down and listen to me." The inspector said, giving the bottle of water to Akashi."

"I have not only come here to give this piece of information to you, but also to apologize on my team's behalf. We searched your house that day and accused you of sheltering Arjun."

Akashi looked at the Inspector, speechless and perplexed.

"Why are you apologizing, Sir? You were doing your duty." Vihaan intervened, in order to extract more information.

The Inspector looked at Vihaan skeptically and then looked at Akashi.

"According to our sources, Arjun died on the evening we arrested the two drug traffickers at Delo. We thought he was missing but later found out that he died by falling off the cliff during a fight." The inspector explained.

"What? How is this possible? Ipsha told me that…"

Vihaan squeezed Akashi's hand as she was about to divulge unnecessary information.

"We got the post-mortem reports of Arjun this morning. Here is a copy of the report. You can have a look. And here are also some pictures of Arjun's body. I am sure these will make the picture clear."

Akashi looked at the photographs of Arjun's rotten dead body, lying on the grassy abyss. Vihaan went through the post-mortem report in detail.

"I am sorry we misbehaved with you and your sister that night. Your father was my teacher. That is the primary reason I wanted to meet you and apologize for that night. I hope your sister recovers soon. There is nothing to worry." The inspector said and got up from the chair.

"Can I know who are you, young man?" The inspector asked Vihaan.

"A family friend," Vihaan replied. The inspector patted his back and left the cafeteria.

"Am I dreaming? This doesn't make any sense." Akashi

mumbled.

"No, you are not. This is the reality. Arjun had died long back. The post-mortem report and the photographs are the proof."

"Then, who was hiding in my house? Whom did Ipsha try to save from the police? And whom did Ipsha talk to, in front of you? Why is Ipsha trying to fool us, Vihaan?" Akashi asked.

"I can't understand. The fog has cleared but the mist has not gone. We can get the answers only from Ipsha." Vihaan replied.

"Things are so complicated. What is happening, Vihaan? Why is my sister deceiving me?"

"I am with you, Akashi. You don't have to do this alone. Let's face it together. Let's get the answers to the countless questions which are killing our sanity." Vihaan said, caressing Akashi's cheek which was moist with her tears.

Akashi looked into Vihaan's eyes and felt relieved that she doesn't have to do this all alone. Her eyes conveyed gratitude to Vihaan. They walked towards Ipsha's room with the hope that the mist would clear. They knew that things would start making sense once Ipsha tells them the truth.

IN RUINS

"There is a secret side to all of us that we shield from everyone. Even if you are very close to someone, there can be something that you don't know about him or her."

Akashi and Vihaan walked into Ipsha's room. They found her smiling as she talked over the phone.

Akashi snatched the phone from Ipsha. She looked at it and saw that no one was on hold. Ipsha was talking to herself.

"What are you doing, Akashi? Give my phone back to me." Ipsha shrieked.

"With whom were you talking, Ipsha?"

"Watch your manners, Akashi. You have never snatched my phone from me in this way." Ipsha looked at her sister, flabbergasted.

"No one is on the other side of the phone. The recent call list shows no incoming or outgoing calls that lasted for a minute. Why are you doing this useless drama? Why are you deceiving us?" Akashi asked, pointing at the mobile screen.

"Stop imagining things. Leave me alone. I can't tolerate

you these days." Ipsha said and took her phone from Akashi's hand.

"I know, but that doesn't mean you will do such nonsense." Akashi retorted.

"Arjun might not make sense to you, but he makes a lot of sense to me. He said he will try to meet me soon. I was happy, but you can't see my happiness even for a minute. " Ipsha said with disgust.

"Arjun is dead, Ipsha. He fell off the cliff and died one week before." Vihaan said.

"Vihaan, you too? I knew Akashi was against me, but you have also started playing games with me." Ipsha said in anger.

"We are not playing games with you, Ipsha. You are playing games with us." Akashi yelled.

"See these photographs, Ipsha. The police gave it to us today. Arjun had died a week before." Vihaan said, handing over the photographs to Ipsha.

Ipsha looked at the photographs for some time with furrowed eyebrows. Then, she returned the photographs to Vihaan without reacting.

"These are fake photographs, Vihaan. Arjun was with me that day. We came home together. I talked to Arjun. He will meet me soon. Akashi has hatched this disgusting plan with the police to separate me from Arjun. Trust me, Vihaan." Ipsha said, looking at Akashi with rage.

Akashi was shocked at the sudden accusation. She was about to say something when Vihaan signaled her to keep quiet.

"Dear Ipsha, I would have agreed with you if I had not checked this report. I know your sister was against your relationship with Arjun. Your anger is reasonable." Vihaan said.

"Vihaan, trust me. This is all Akashi's plan. After you left her, she was very lonely and depressed. She could not bear it that Arjun and I are so happy in our relationship. She always had pride in her beauty. I admit she is way more beautiful than me, but Arjun loved me. Arjun told me that Akashi is interested in him. She had met him in his hotel one morning without telling me. But Arjun never gave in to her tricks. Arjun only loves me." Ipsha said confidently.

"Stop it, Ipsha. What rubbish are you speaking? How can you think that I was interested in Arjun? Your thoughts are so nasty." Akashi winced. Vihaan signaled her to keep quiet.

"I have also seen the post-mortem report of Arjun. You check it yourself. Arjun is no more." Vihaan said giving the report to Ipsha.

"Listen, Arjun will meet me soon. I talked to him today. Don't play these games with me. I don't need to see anything as I know that these reports and photographs are not real. Get lost! Get out of here!" Ipsha tore the report into pieces without giving it a look. She started throwing things around her and screamed.

The nurses rushed into her room and injected her cleverly. She dozed off soon. Akashi and Vihaan stood there, stunned as they watched Ipsha in ruins.

**

Akashi showed the photographs and post-mortem report of Arjun to Dr. Sharma. He told her that Dr. Sen, a renowned psychiatrist of Darjeeling would be in the hospital by evening. He would be doing Ipsha's treatment.

Akashi nodded. She had never felt so battered, vulnerable and bruised in life. She could not figure out why Ipsha was deceiving her in this manner. She can no longer tolerate Ipsha's hatred for her. Every day, she hopes that tomorrow would be better, but the darkness increases without any mercy. *Is hope nothing but a lie?* She had started questioning herself.

"Hold on to hope for some more time." Vihaan held her hand and said. Akashi looked at him and wondered how he could read her mind.

"Let's go home. Take some rest. Ipsha is sleeping under the effect of the injection. The nurses are there to look after her. We will come in the evening." Vihaan suggested.

Akashi agreed and they walked home together. She entered her room and sat on the bed. She told Vihaan to not disturb her as she needed some time to think. Vihaan understood and decided to watch TV in the living room.

Akashi thought about the sketches of Ipsha that she had discovered the other day. She took the bunch of sketches and started studying them. Each sketch had a little write-up on it.

The first sketch was that of a man walking in the woods. The man wore a hat and had a harmonica in his hand.

Who are you, robbing my sanity with your mysterious presence?

The second sketch was that of a pair of eyes watching a girl from the window while she is asleep.

I know I am being constantly watched by you. Yes, I am scared, but this is a sweet fear. I am addicted to it.

The next sketch was that of a girl walking with her friends. A man wearing a hat is watching her from behind a tree.

I wonder if I am enjoying or despising getting stalked by you. When will you come in front of me?

The fourth sketch was that of a girl and the hat man looking at each other.

Finally, I met you. It was the most beautiful moment of my life. I am all yours.

The next sketch was that of a girl and a guy dancing closely. Someone is playing a violin beside them.

Our first date! You make me feel beautiful.

The next sketch was that of a girl playing the synthesizer and a guy sitting beside her. Another girl was sitting a little far from them.

Akashi and Arjun sang together. I was happy until Arjun started praising her. Why does Akashi always take the limelight from me? She has been doing this with me from as long as I can remember.

The next sketch was that of a couple facing the Watershed View Point.

This day changed our lives forever. Arjun and I came so close to each other. Akashi finds faults in him because she doesn't want me to be happy in this relationship.

The next sketch was that of a couple embracing each other.

I feel so peaceful when I am in his arms. For the first time, someone made me feel special and beautiful. Akashi has always been the cherry of everyone's eyes. I have always thought myself to be the ugly sibling and Akashi to be the pretty one.

Akashi sighed and drank some water. She was shocked to know that Ipsha had such a complex. She moved to the next sketch where a girl and a boy were paragliding.

The best moment of my life was flying in the sky with my love.

The next sketch was that of a guy fighting with some men beside a cliff. A girl is standing at the corner.

Fear sheaths the place. They kept on beating him. There was blood everywhere. Finally, I could see Arjun again. My Arjun is very strong. I could finally take him to my house and he is with me now.

Akashi felt nauseous after studying the sketches. She learnt various facets of Ipsha that were unknown to her all these days.

Despite being so close to Ipsha, I hardly understood her.

She summoned Vihaan and showed him the sketches.

"We must show these sketches to Dr. Sen. It can help in Ipsha's treatment." Vihaan said after looking at the sketches. Akashi was lost in her thoughts as she understood from where everything began.

"Why did Arjun come into our lives, Vihaan? He came like a typhoon and messed up our beautiful, little world." Akashi cried out.

"Will I be able to rescue Ipsha from the dilapidated condition? Will I be able to bring her back to normal life?

Will she love me again?" Akashi asked Vihaan amid her sobs.

"Yes, you can do that. You are very strong with a high willpower. I am confident you will bring back Ipsha to life again. Ipsha loves you a lot, Akashi. Everything will be fine." Vihaan said, looking into Akashi's eyes. He knew that Akashi can go to any length to cure Ipsha.

BROKEN PIECES OF GLASS

"The wounds on our loved one's body produce the equal number of invisible wounds in our heart."

After having lunch, Akashi and Vihaan headed towards the hospital. Akashi took Ipsha's sketches along with her so that she could show them to the doctor. They learnt that Dr. Sen has arrived from Darjeeling and is waiting for them. They walked in Dr. Sharma's cabin where the two doctors were discussing about Ipsha's health.

"It is risky to keep her here." Dr. Sen said to Dr. Sharma.

"I agree, but you have to talk to the patient's guardian. Oh, there she is! Ipsha's elder sister." Dr. Sharma said, pointing at Akashi.

Akashi could comprehend that Ipsha's condition was not good. She heaved a sigh and prepared herself to listen to the truth.

"How is Ipsha?" She asked the doctors.

"Where are Ipsha's parents?" The doctor asked.

"Mom and Dad had passed away in an accident many years back. Since then, I am her only guardian." Akashi said softly.

"And who is this young man?" The doctor asked.

"Her fiancé." Vihaan declared before Akashi could say anything. Akashi looked at Vihaan with surprise, unaware of where it had come from. Vihaan smiled at her and looked at the doctor.

"Good that Ipsha has both of you in such a dark phase of her life. I have studied all her reports. After doing her checkup, I can say that she is not at all well." Dr. Sen said.

"What has exactly happened to her? Dr. Sharma said that she is in trauma." Akashi asked.

"Not mere trauma, Miss Akashi. Ipsha is suffering from post-traumatic schizophrenia and she is in the chronic stage." The doctor said, emphasizing on each word.

The mention of schizophrenia shocked both Akashi and Vihaan. They looked at each other in disbelief.

"Arjun died in front of her eyes that day. Ipsha couldn't bear the shock of Arjun's death. As a result, her mind started conjuring an unreal world from that time. She started believing that Arjun is alive. She did not lie about Arjun staying in your house. She said it because she could see Arjun. She was in that unreal world where Arjun was alive and with her in her room. Her mind made her visualize that Arjun had to escape her room when the police came in search of him. After that, she attempted suicide because she believed that you separated her from Arjun.

She can hear and see Arjun even now. That's the reason you might find her talking to Arjun over the phone. That's what I noticed when I went for her checkup. She is not lying or creating a drama. She is suffering from chronic psychosis where her mind has lost contact with reality. Her overall personality had undergone huge changes because of this. You must have noticed it." The doctor paused.

"Yes. She always blames me and hates me these days. She loved me the most in this world. Now, she hates me so much." Akashi said with anguish.

"She is not doing it on her own. Her mind is making her do that. The most common symptoms of schizophrenia are auditory and visual hallucinations accompanied with unclear thinking." The doctor said.

"So, she didn't believe that Arjun had died when we showed her the photographs and the post-mortem report." Vihaan said.

"Exactly. It is not only hard but impossible to make Ipsha realize the difference between the real world and the unreal world that she has created. The more you would try to make her understand, the more she would get aggressive. In the process, she can hurt herself badly like she has done earlier." The doctor explained.

"So, she is suffering from schizophrenia after she saw Arjun die in front of her eyes." Akashi asked.

"Most probably. It caused her immense shock and pain. She might have slipped into depression for a few hours after that incident. Her mind then started conjuring this unreal world." The doctor said with a thoughtful look.

Akashi remembered that Ipsha came back home and locked herself inside her room the entire night. The next day, in the late afternoon, when the news flashed that Arjun is missing, Ipsha told her that Arjun is in her room.

"Miss Akashi, did Ipsha suffer from any severe trauma in her childhood?" The doctor asked, interrupting her thoughts.

"She was only twelve when she saw the mutilated body of our parents. She did not shed a single drop of tear, but she ran away from the place. I remember I used to hold her and cry for hours, but she never cried. She never mentioned Mom and Dad in our conversations until a year passed by." Akashi recollected.

"Anything else? Think. Did anyone bully or abuse her when she was a child?" The doctor asked.

"She was very thin and tomboyish when she was around thirteen or fourteen. Many people used to call her Lanky

149

Panky, Lady's Finger etc. Her classmates used to bully her saying that she is so thin. Our neighbors used to tell her that I was feminine and pretty, whereas she is a tomboy. They used to tell her to be like me." Akashi recalled.

"I was wondering all this while how Ipsha became a patient of chronic schizophrenia all of a sudden. But now, the things seem clear." The doctor said.

Akashi stared at the doctor, waiting for him to speak.

"Ipsha had suffered many traumas in her childhood. The news of her parent's death and seeing the maimed body of her parents took her to a denial stage. She was not ready to accept that her parents were no more. An entire year took her to believe and accept it."

As the doctor said these words, Akashi recollected how Ipsha used to draw her happy family in her drawing book even after their parent's death. Akashi did not pay heed to it that time.

"The bullying that she faced made her feel lonely and unwanted. She had a low self esteem and a complex that she was not beautiful. Deep in her heart, she always wanted someone who would love her. She wanted a person who would make her feel beautiful and loved. This is the reason she got attracted to Arjun and became crazy for him. The bottom line is Ipsha had always been suffering from some amount of schizophrenia, but no one could understand." The doctor said.

The doctor's words left Akashi flabbergasted. She realized why Ipsha loved fantasy fiction. She also created various unreal worlds in her canvas. She escaped to an unreal world whenever she felt sad.

Ipsha sketched Arjun in a black hat and a black robe. But Akashi had never seen Arjun dress like that. There was also a harmonica in the sketches. Ipsha told Akashi that Arjun impressed her by playing a tune on his harmonica. But she had never heard Arjun playing the harmonica. Does it mean that the hat and the harmonica were a figment of Ipsha's imagination? Her sketches show an unreal world that she had built for herself. Perhaps, she builds the unreal world in her canvas and then gets into it.

Akashi felt dizzy with her own thoughts. She made a mental note to check Ipsha's room for the love notes that Arjun had sent to her.

Akashi told the doctor everything that hit her mind and showed him all the sketches of Ipsha. The doctor responded with a nod.

Suddenly, two nurses rushed inside the cabin saying that they cannot control Ipsha. Her behavior is weird and aggressive. The doctors along with Akashi and Vihaan ran to Ipsha's room. They saw Ipsha sitting with open arms and closed eyes as if she is hugging someone.

"Ipsha!" Akashi called.

"Please don't call the police, Akashi. Arjun will go just now. I love Arjun. I can't live without him." Ipsha said, crying as she saw so many people gathered in her room.

"Arjun is nowhere in this room dear." Akashi said.

"Have you become blind? I was hugging him ten seconds back and you say you cannot see him. You know you have become mad." Ipsha giggled.

Akashi looked at Dr. Sen who approached Ipsha. Suddenly, Ipsha's expression changed to sadness.

"Don't go away Arjun. This is my doctor, not the police." Ipsha cried out.

"Why are you doing this to me? I can't live without Arjun. Why can't you people understand?" Anger took over Ipsha and she started shouting.

Dr. Sen tried to calm her but to no avail. She shouted as much as she could with her frail body. The nurse offered a glass of water to her which she threw at once. Her shrieks continued until weakness took over. She shivered and fell, unconscious on the broken pieces of glass lying on the floor.

Blood oozed from her hands as she lay there senseless. The nurses lifted her to bed and bandaged her wounds.

The broken pieces of glass did not only hurt Ipsha but also managed to produce the equal number of scars in Akashi's heart. Akashi could feel a terrible pain in her chest. She could not see her little sister in such a pathetic condition.

EYE-OPENER

"We, humans love to play the blame game. Sometimes, we put the blame on our foes, other times on our loved ones and the worst, at times on ourselves. Before acceptance, we often take refuge in the canopy of the blame."

Vihaan was surprised to see Akashi running towards home.

"What's there at home?" Vihaan asked, but Akashi did not reply.

As they reached home, Akashi walked into Ipsha's room and searched every nook and corner.

"What are you searching? Tell me, Akashi."

"The love notes that Arjun had sent Ipsha to woo her." Akashi said.

Vihaan understood what was going in Akashi's mind. Without saying anything, he too started searching. Even after fifteen minutes, they couldn't find any of the love notes.

"Perhaps she had thrown them," Vihaan said.

Suddenly, Akashi's eyes went to Ipsha's school bag that was kept at the corner of her study table.

"I found the notes, Vihaan," Akashi shouted as she looked inside the bag.

They took out a dozen of white folded pieces of paper from the bag.

"Let's see what is written in these notes," Vihaan said to Akashi. Her heart was pounding.

Both of them started unfolding the pieces of paper one by one, but to their surprise, there was nothing written on them. They could not find a single mark of ink on any of the papers. They were blank.

"How can it be?" Vihaan muttered.

"Arjun did not send Ipsha any love note. These are all figments of her imagination." Akashi said and sat on the chair, exhausted.

"You mean she imagined that Arjun had sent her love notes to woo her." Vihaan said, fumbling.

"The notes, the harmonica, the hat….everything is unreal. Didn't you hear the doctor say that Ipsha has always been schizophrenic?"

"How could you never understand it, Akashi?"

"I don't know, Vihaan. I feel so sorry for everything."

"So, in Ipsha and Arjun's story, most of the things are made up in Ipsha's mind," Vihaan said trying to make sense of the situation.

"Arjun existed. I have met him. He told me that he loves Ipsha. That's real too. He used to stalk me as he doubted that he had left something in my bag. I guess Ipsha had seen him around our house and then she started living in a fantasy. Arjun fell in love with her and they dated, but Ipsha added more matter to it through her imagination. The harmonica, the hat and the love notes never existed in this story. They only existed in Ipsha's mind." Akashi said.

Both Akashi and Vihaan sat in silence for an hour.

"I am not a good sister. I couldn't take care of Ipsha." Akashi uttered.

"Hey! Stop blaming yourself. I know all these eye-opening facts are too tough to accept, but that doesn't mean you will blame yourself." Vihaan said.

"My sister had been suffering from a mental disease and I could not understand. If Mom and Dad were alive today, they would have surely understood." Akashi said, sobbing. Vihaan wrapped his arms around her and kissed her forehead.

"Ipsha is under Dr. Sen's treatment now. She will get well soon." Vihaan said, wiping her tears.

Akashi looked at him and nodded.

"And I am with you." Vihaan said with a smile. It calmed Akashi's restless mind.

**

"Doctor, please do something. I cannot see my sister in this condition. How long will it take for her to recover?" Akashi asked the doctor.

Earlier, she was clueless about Ipsha's behavior. She assumed that Arjun had influenced Ipsha to behave badly with her. After knowing that Ipsha is schizophrenic, there is only sorrow and remorse in her heart.

"Miss D'Souza, please calm down. This is the time when only patience and prayers can help you. More than the schizophrenic patient, the ones who get the most affected are the caregivers. I can understand your state of mind. I want to tell you that there is hope. Ipsha will be fine. Yes, it will take time, may be a lot of time, but she will make it." The doctor paused.

Vihaan clutched Akashi's hand.

"The first thing that I would suggest is take Ipsha to a different place. If possible, please relocate somewhere away from the hills. The new ambiance will keep Ipsha away from Arjun's memories. The more Ipsha would see familiar places, the more her mind would conjure up stories of Arjun. A new place and meeting new people will help her recover." The

155

doctor said.

"Where should I move with Ipsha, doctor?" Akashi asked, clueless.

"Move to Kolkata or any other city. The environment is completely different. Moreover, the treatment facilities and counseling sessions are much better in a city. Look, schizophrenia demands lifelong treatment. Even when the symptoms will subside in Ipsha, you have to screen her constantly so that she doesn't develop them again. Right now, I am prescribing some injections because Ipsha won't take the antipsychotic pills. After a week, I will replace the injection with the pills. The pills and injections will control the symptoms. However, along with it you must ensure that Ipsha gets proper food and adequate sleep."

Akashi nodded.

"Have faith in the Divine. Her medication has started and the extreme symptoms of psychosis will soon recede. You see if you can move to some other place." Dr. Sen said.

CHANGE IS THE ONLY CONSTANT

"Life is wiser than us and sometimes, we should blindly trust life to show us the way."

Akashi and Vihaan walked out of the doctor's cabin. Akashi was worried about where she should relocate with Ipsha.

As they came outside the hospital, Vihaan held her hand and asked, "What are you thinking?"

"About everything the doctor said. I am clueless about where I should move with Ipsha. I have to quit my job and sell my house which is the only sign of Mom and Dad. I don't have enough funds to settle in a new city. So, I have to sell the house." Akashi said in distress.

"You and Ipsha are coming to Delhi with me. Both of you will stay at my house. Don't even think of selling your house. You can look for a job in Delhi. I am sure there are better facilities for Ipsha's treatment in Delhi." Vihaan said.

"What will your parents say, Vihaan? I am a friend of yours. I don't want to burden you with my problems. You are already doing so much for me in my dark days. Please don't keep me in debts." Akashi said.

"You must have forgotten what I told Dr. Sen when he asked me who I am. Anyways, to make matters simple, let me say directly to you. I love you, Akashi. Will you marry me?" Vihaan asked without any delay. Akashi was taken aback by the question. She couldn't believe her eyes.

"Please stop it, Vihaan. I don't want to be an object of your pity. I know how detached and happy-go-lucky you are. You have always hated the concept of marriage. I know you are doing all this because I am in such a terrible state. I beg you, Vihaan. Don't love or marry me because you sympathize with my condition." Akashi said.

"Trust me, Akashi. I am not doing this for pity or anything else. I am doing this because I love you and I want to be with you in all your ups and downs. I am doing this because your sister is my sister and I want to take care of her along with you. I walked away from the relationship because I thought I was not good enough for you. I thought you deserve better. The separation from you made me realize what a fool I had been. I should have worked on the relationship, not walked away from it." Vihaan said with sincerity. Akashi could feel that his words were genuine. However, she looked away and started walking.

"Akashi, wait. Give an answer to my proposal." Vihaan said.

Akashi felt vulnerable as she looked at him.

Vihaan held her close and asked, kissing her forehead, "Will you marry me, Akashi?"

Akashi nodded and asked, "But what about your parents?"

"They adore you. They will like my decision." Vihaan said.

Akashi felt it was a miracle. The person who chose to walk away from her life walked into her life again at the most crucial hour, when she needed a support. If Vihaan wouldn't have been with her, Akashi knew that she couldn't handle the truth.

God never closes a door without opening another one. This incident restored Akashi's faith in miracles.

**

Akashi was feeding cheese sandwiches to Ipsha in the hospital. After a week of medication, Ipsha was a little better. She no longer overreacts, but she has become detached. She does not eat unless she is fed. She does not sleep unless she is put to sleep. She never talks on her own unless someone initiates a conversation with her. She does not sketch and doesn't watch television even when it is switched on. She is unusually quiet and detached from the world.

"Why is Ipsha not speaking a word?" Akashi asked the doctor.

"The medicines have taken care of the dangerous symptoms, but she has retreated into a shell. She needs proper counseling." The doctor said.

"Where can I give her counseling sessions?" Akashi asked.

"Vihaan told me that you are relocating to New Delhi next week."

"Yes."

"Excellent. I will write a letter to Dr. Shergill. He will take care of Ipsha. He has a center for the treatment of schizophrenia patients where patients get therapy, social skills training and supported employment. The center also provides education and support to the families dealing with such patients." Dr. Sen elaborated.

"Thank you so much doctor. Will Ipsha be fine with medication and regular counseling?" Akashi asked with a renewed hope.

"Definitely! She will be doing fine. But yes, do remember that individuals with schizophrenia need support, patience, and empathy. You have to look after her always." The doctor explained

"I will take care of her always. She is the most important person in my life." Akashi said.

"I am putting her on antipsychotic pills instead of injections from today." The doctor said.

The path seemed clear to Akashi. It's not that the tempest has gone but Akashi knew where she was heading and what needs to be done. The fear of the unknown is more dangerous than the fear of darkness.

Akashi was sad about leaving the beautiful and serene town of Kalimpong. But she also knew that change is the only constant. Only change can make things better for Ipsha and her.

"Is Ipsha fine?" Vihaan asked as Akashi walked inside the house.

"Better, but quiet," Akashi replied.

"She will be fine soon," Vihaan said with a smile. "But why do you look lost?"

"I have to leave this house, this town which bears so many memories." Akashi said.

"Delhi is too hot in the summers. I promise you that we will be holidaying here every summer. Life is not only about holding on to memories, but it is also about new experiences and creating new memories." Vihaan said. His words drew a smile on Akashi's face.

"I love your smile. We will get engaged as soon as we reach Delhi. Then, whenever you think the situation is right, we will get married." Vihaan said, beaming.

"Thanks for everything," Akashi said.

"Why do you keep saying thanks, Akashi? Instead, you can say that you love me." Vihaan said with a wink.

"You know I do." Akashi smiled.

A New Leaf

"Life is like a seasonal circle. There is a time when you suffer loss and become bare like the autumn. Then, there comes a time when the pain intensifies to such an extent that you feel numb, like the winter. Finally, after a lot of anguish, beauty returns in life again like the colorful spring."

A new chapter began in the life of Akashi and Ipsha after they relocated to Delhi. Akashi handed over the maintenance of their house to Malati Masi and her family. It was painful to go away from Kalimpong, their house, and Malati Masi, but it was essential for Ipsha's well-being.

Vihaan's parents welcomed them with warmth and love. Akashi and Vihaan got engaged in a small family ceremony after a week of reaching Delhi. Akashi decided to get married only after Ipsha's health gets better.

Ipsha became unbelievably quiet. She hardly talks to anyone. She is no longer the chirpy and effervescent girl that she had always been. Her treatment and counseling sessions are going well under Dr. Shergill. She is provided with therapy and social skills training. Dr. Shergill said that it would take about a year for her to talk and mingle with people freely.

One evening, as Akashi went in her room, she saw Ipsha sketching something on her canvas.

"My Ipsha is sketching today. Let me see what she is sketching." Akashi said with a bright smile and neared Ipsha to see what she had drawn on her canvas.

To her surprise, Akashi saw that Ipsha had again drawn Arjun. This has become a daily ritual since a week. Ever since Ipsha had started drawing after reaching Delhi, all she draws is Arjun. Sometimes Arjun is in a black hat and a black robe, some other times he is in a casual outfit. In some sketches, Arjun is gazing at her from a distance, whereas in some others, Arjun and Ipsha are holding hands.

"What is this, Ipsha?" Akashi asked.

"Sketch." Ipsha replied without any expression.

"I know that. But whose sketch is this?" Akashi asked further.

"Arjun." Ipsha replied.

"Where is Arjun?"

"I don't know. I want to go home." Ipsha yelped.

"This is our home, baby." Akashi said, cuddling Ipsha.

"No. The old home. In the hills. Arjun must be there waiting for me. I want to go there." Ipsha started sobbing and it took more than fifteen minutes for Akashi to calm her.

**

When the same thing continued for over a month, Akashi showed all the sketches to Dr. Shergill.

"That's more than a hundred sketches." Dr. Shergill said.

"Yes! 100 sketches in one month. She makes sketches of Arjun the entire day. She doesn't talk about him, but she has kept him alive in her canvas."

"I must say that Ipsha is a brilliant artist. Why don't you admit her in an art school? She will learn to paint and sketch some new things. It will probably keep Arjun's thoughts

162

away from her mind and canvas. As we can see, Ipsha's mind and canvas are interwoven." Dr. Shergill said as he studied the sketches.

"But doctor, there will be so many students in the art school. Ipsha is socially awkward. Will it be safe to send her to an art school?" Akashi asked.

"The chronic symptoms have gone. The counseling sessions that we are providing will help her to interact with people. At least, it is better than staying at home all day. She can make some friends there." Dr. Shergill said.

Akashi looked lost.

"Give it some time. Arjun is very much alive in her memories. It will take some time for Ipsha to let go of it. So, we need to keep her distracted. Joining an art school will be a good thing for her as we cannot resume her education right now. Keeping her at home all day will definitely not help her to get back to normal life." Dr. Shergill explained.

"Alright, doctor. As you say." Akashi smiled.

**

Akashi admitted Ipsha to an art school located close to their house. When Akashi told Ipsha about it, she smiled without any word. She did not seem interested. On the first day, Vihaan accompanied Akashi and Ipsha to the art school.

Ipsha was nonchalant. She looked here and there after entering the school but didn't speak a word. She was least bothered about her new school. She held Akashi's fingers tightly and followed her.

"Ipsha, you need to go inside your classroom. I am waiting here for you. We will go back home together. Okay, sweetest?" Akashi said, planting a kiss on Ipsha's cheek.

Ipsha looked inside the class and shook her head.

"Don't be scared, darling. You are here to learn and do the thing you love the most: painting." Akashi said with a smile.

"You come inside. I don't know anyone here." Ipsha said.

"You will make new friends in the class. Come on, be a good girl and attend your class. We are waiting for you here." Vihaan said with a cheerful smile.

Finally, Ipsha walked into the classroom reluctantly. The other students were hustling and bustling around her, making her shiver. She quietly took her seat and looked around in nervousness.

As the teacher walked into the class, Ipsha started feeling better. The first lesson was on oil painting. The teacher taught the basic techniques and told the students to create an abstract oil painting.

Ipsha found solace in the class .She grasped the method that the teacher explained and started working on her painting.

The class was still chaotic with the students babbling and giggling, but Ipsha was busy with her canvas. Right at that moment, she heard a voice, "Hey! Hi! Hello there!"

Ipsha turned around to find a boy of her age, smiling at her.

"I am calling you since such a long time. It seems you are crazy about art. I mean no one in this class is as engrossed in painting as you are, not even the teacher." He said and laughed at his own words.

Ipsha didn't understand what was so amusing about it. After all, Akashi had admitted her in the school so that she can learn arts.

She checked out the guy in front of her. He looked bubbling in high spirits in a red angry bird T-shirt and geek glasses. Ipsha noticed that he is tall and has a cheerful countenance. She turned back without a word.

"Hey, hello! wait!" The guy jumped from his seat to Ipsha's seat as Ipsha turned back.

"What are you doing?" Ipsha asked, aghast.

"Trying to talk to you. Listen, you have to share your oil paints with me and also help me with the painting." The guy said in a cordial way as if he and Ipsha have been friends since childhood.

"Sorry. I don't share things with strangers." Ipsha said and concentrated on her canvas.

"Stranger? Who? Me? We are in the same class, miss. So, even if we are not friends, we are classmates. We will be meeting every day. I can assure you that you will be dying to be my best friend after a few days. After all, I am such a charmer." The guy smiled.

"Why haven't you brought your own stuff to the class?" Ipsha asked with annoyance.

"Why do you frown so often? You have such a cute face. You should smile." The guy said.

Ipsha did not reply. She turned her face away.

"Hey, miss. I am sorry." The guy said, holding his ears. Ipsha couldn't help smiling.

"Actually, I am not interested in Arts. That's the excuse I gave to my family so that they stop forcing me to appear in the JEE examinations. You seem to be a professional artist." The guy said.

"Thanks." Ipsha smiled.

"Friends?" The guy extended his hand towards Ipsha.

"Ipsha," Ipsha said as she shook hands with him.

"Arjun." The guy said, making Ipsha speechless.

Ipsha gazed at his face as Arjun kept on speaking about his life with enthusiasm.

Epilogue

Eight months later

Today is Akashi and Vihaan's wedding. After relocating to Delhi, Akashi saw Vihaan in a new light. He doesn't run away from his responsibilities anymore. He deeply cares for her and Ipsha. She wondered if it was the separation or the challenging circumstances that resulted in the change.

"Akashi!" Ipsha walked inside Akashi's room as Akashi was getting ready.

"You look so beautiful," Ipsha said. Akashi blushed and pinched Ipsha's cheeks.

"Here is a present for you. Please open it." Ipsha gave the gift and waited with excitement to see Akashi's reaction.

Akashi was surprised to find that it was a beautiful oil painting of her and Vihaan.

"This is marvelous, Ipsha. I loved it so much. I am sure Vihaan would love it even more." Akashi said, marveling at the art work.

"Thank you. Arjun had helped me a lot in preparing this gift. We both made it together." Ipsha said with a smile.

"Ahem!" Akashi teased Ipsha.

Ipsha blushed and said, "He is my friend, Akashi."

"Arjun really likes you. Hope you know that." Akashi said, caressing Ipsha's cheek.

"Akashi, why are we talking about this? Today is your day. Get ready soon. Vihaan is waiting for you." Ipsha said and went out of the room with a smile.

Akashi was happy to see Ipsha like this. A few months back, she thought that she had lost Ipsha forever. With proper medication and counseling, Ipsha has recovered to a huge extent. And then Arjun came into Ipsha's life like the brightest ray of hope.

It is strange that a certain Arjun messed up Ipsha's life and left her in ruins. And then, another Arjun came into her life and stitched back her broken pieces. Ever since Ipsha met Arjun at her art school, things have moved towards the better. Both of them became good friends in a short span of time. Arjun's chirpy and energetic nature has helped Ipsha to come out of her shell. The new Arjun has helped Ipsha to slowly forget the old Arjun.

Dr. Shergill was happy to see the progress in Ipsha's health. He warned Akashi and Vihaan to never take Ipsha to Kalimpong anytime soon. He said that past incidents can play a trick on Ipsha's mind if she is exposed to the old ambiance. He also told Akashi and Vihaan to throw away the sketches that Ipsha had made earlier. He said not to keep anything that can remind Ipsha of Arjun.

Akashi is fond of the new Arjun in Ipsha's life. She feels that their parents, in the form of Guardian Angels have helped Ipsha to get back to normal life. No one could have imagined Ipsha to come back from the hellish cave where she was residing a few months back.

Akashi is forever grateful to Vihaan. Had Vihaan not come to Kalimpong after hearing that Ipsha was in the hospital, Akashi couldn't have managed things alone. It was because of Vihaan that Akashi could save Ipsha and herself from getting drowned. It was Vihaan's motivation which helped her to get a job as an assistant professor in a reputed college of Delhi.

Akashi ruminated that Vihaan is not only her lover and her husband to be, but her best friend. When the foundation of love is friendship, it neither changes, nor lessens any day. It stays the same: evergreen, beautiful and solacing. This is the reason that even after the break up, Akashi couldn't find any emotional distance between Vihaan and her.

Akashi looked at the painting and felt blessed for having Vihaan by her side. Her reverie got interrupted by Ipsha's voice, asking her whether she is ready.

ABOUT THE AUTHOR

Purba Chakraborty is a novelist, poet, web content developer, lifestyle blogger and social influencer from Kolkata. She has authored two novels "Walking in the streets of love and destiny", "The Hidden Letters" and a poetry book "The Heart Listens to No One". "Canvas of a Mind" is her third novel. Her short stories and poems have been published in more than ten anthologies and various magazines.

She lives with her father and grandmother. Her hobbies are reading, singing and traveling. Books and music are her most loved companions. She plans a vacation every few months to a beach or a hill station. Her wanderlust is insatiable. She believes that traveling makes her a better storyteller as she comes across so many fascinating people during travelling. She is a restless dreamer and wishes to write till her last breath.

She blogs regularly at Love, Laugh and Reflect (www.purba-chakraborty.com)

She can be reached at:
Facebook: writerpurbachakraborty
Twitter: @Manchali_Purba
Instagram: purba_chakraborty
email: purba.khushi@gmail.com